Buenos Aires Docs

Finding the prescription for a love that lasts...

Meet the dedicated medics of the Hospital General de Buenos Aires. They might be winners in their work, but they all need a little help when it comes to finding their happy-ever-afters!

Luckily for them, passion is sweeping through the corridors of the hospital like a virus and no one is immune! Are they brave enough to take their chance on happiness...and each other?

Find out in

Sebastián and Isabella's story
ER Doc's Miracle Triplets by Tina Beckett

Carlos and Sofia's story
Surgeon's Brooding Brazilian Rival by Luana DaRosa

Available now!

Gabriel and Ana's story
Daring to Fall for the Single Dad by Becky Wicks

Felipe and Emilia's story
Secretly Dating the Baby Doc by JC Harroway

Coming next month!

Dear Reader,

When I first started my writing adventure, I never dreamed I would someday have fifty published books. And yet here I am. And the surprising thing is that the ideas still come—almost faster than I can write them at times. I love being able to tell stories. And yet it sometimes becomes complicated in ways I never imagined.

Such is what happens with the characters of this book. Isabella wanted something so badly that she almost sacrificed everything for it. And when she gets it...well, let's just say things get complicated. Thank you so much for joining Seb and Bella as they try to figure out if their relationship is worth saving after the heartbreak of IVF treatments that failed time and time again. But there's a surprise in store for them. I hope you love discovering what that surprise is as much as I loved writing these two special characters. Enjoy!

Love,

Tina Beckett

ER DOC'S MIRACLE TRIPLETS

TINA BECKETT

Special thanks and acknowledgment are given to Tina Beckett for her contribution to the Buenos Aires Docs miniseries.

Recycling programs for this product may not exist in your area.

ISBN-13: 978-1-335-59552-2

ER Doc's Miracle Triplets

For questions and comments about the quality of this book, please contact us at CustomerService@Harlequin.com.

Harlequin Enterprises ULC
22 Adelaide St. West, 41st Floor
Toronto, Ontario M5H 4E3, Canada
www.Harlequin.com

Printed in U.S.A.

Three-time Golden Heart® Award finalist **Tina Beckett** learned to pack her suitcases almost before she learned to read. Born to a military family, she has lived in the United States, Puerto Rico, Portugal and Brazil. In addition to traveling, Tina loves to cuddle with her pug, Alex; spend time with her family; and hit the trails on her horse. Learn more about Tina from her website or friend her on Facebook.

Books by Tina Beckett

Harlequin Medical Romance

California Nurses

The Nurse's One-Night Baby

Starting Over with the Single Dad
Their Reunion to Remember
One Night with the Sicilian Surgeon
From Wedding Guest to Bride?
A Family Made in Paradise
The Vet, the Pup and the Paramedic
The Surgeon She Could Never Forget
Resisting the Brooding Heart Surgeon
A Daddy for the Midwife's Twins?
Tempting the Off-Limits Nurse

Visit the Author Profile page
at Harlequin.com for more titles.

To my wonderful family!

Praise for
Tina Beckett

"Tina Beckett definitely followed through on the premise and managed to infuse just the right amount of angst and passion to keep me glued to the pages of *Miracle Baby for the Midwife* from beginning to end."

—*Harlequin Junkie*

PROLOGUE

"BELLA...*QUERIDA*. I'M so sorry, but I just can't...with any of it. We agreed this would be the last time." Sebastián held a sheaf of papers in his hand.

She bowed her head and stared at the dining room table, willing herself not to cry over her latest loss. *Their* latest loss. She knew they'd agreed. Six weeks had passed since their latest attempt at IVF had ended with her spotting again. It had followed the same pattern for the last couple of years: implanting the embryos only to start bleeding a week or two later and hear she'd lost them. Their doctor had even tried a new regimen of hormones, hoping that she would be able to retain the pregnancy this time.

It was obvious she hadn't. Again. Even though she'd held on to it for weeks longer this time.

Seb wasn't telling her anything she didn't

already know. And although he hadn't been cruel and mentioned that they'd both agreed that the time before this one would be the last attempt, he might as well have. Because today he seemed different. Harder, somehow. As if he'd made a decision and was walling himself off from what had happened… walling himself off from *her*. Brick by brick. Layer by layer.

"But…" She forced her teeth to bite down after that single word came out, refusing to beg him for one more attempt.

As if he knew the words were swirling in her brain, even if her lips weren't uttering them, Seb slowly shook his head, a pained tightening of his mouth the only indication of how difficult the gesture was.

She stared down at her hands, knowing he was right. But after all this time…after all of those tries, how could he just…give up?

The fact that he hadn't mentioned adoption or surrogacy like he had after the last failed treatment was telling. Her head came up to look at his face. The gorgeous face of the man she'd loved. The man she'd once burned for with the fire of a thousand *estrellas*.

Once?

No. She still loved him. Desperately. But

when was the last time they'd made love deep into the night? The last time she'd reached for him without the fear of jarring something loose in her womb? Everything had become so timid and fearful and…careful. Her glance shifted back to the papers in his hands and her breath hissed out.

Divorce? Oh, *Dios*, no! She swallowed hard. "W-what are those?"

He didn't even have to ask what she was talking about. "I've accepted a temporary assignment with Médecins sans Frontières." A muscle worked in his cheek. "You need some space, Bella. *We* need some space."

Part of her wanted to sag in relief that he didn't want to end things completely. But wasn't this the same thing? A trial run to see how he would fare without her and her relentless attempts to carry a child? He was probably wildly relieved to get away from her.

Unlike her, who needed him on so many levels. Especially right now. She wanted to shout at him that he needed to stay, needed to at least try to work things out. But she wondered if there was even anything left to work on. So she didn't say any of that. Instead, she simply asked, "When do you leave?"

"Next week."

Next week. So he'd already applied for this position some time ago. How long did it take to be accepted? Had he been busy filling out forms even as they'd implanted the embryos? The thought filled her heart with anger, and bile swept up her throat, leaving an awful taste in her mouth.

"How long will you be gone?"

Did she really want to know?

"I'm contracted for eight weeks in Angola. But it depends on the conditions I find when I arrive."

In other words, he might stay even longer. Her anger went up a notch.

Let him go. He'd already decided all of this without consulting her. Without even asking her if she wanted to go with him. In the back of her mind there was a little nudge. He *had* asked her. A few years ago, when they were still making love with a fervor that left her breathless. When trying to have a baby had actually been filled with adventure and lots of steamy experimentation. Before the desperation had set in. Before they'd turned to fertility specialists and all that it entailed. Yes, he'd asked her about Doctors without Borders, but she'd been too excited at the possibility of being a mom, so she told him to ask her again in a year or two. He never had.

And he evidently wasn't going to.

She hardened her heart against the hurt, against the feelings of abandonment. So yes, let him go. She didn't even ask him where in Angola he was headed. Maybe the separation would reset her system and she'd be able to let go of the dream of having his child once and for all. At forty-one, and after ten years of trying to beat the odds, she knew those odds were now stacked higher than ever against them. And if he decided he wanted a divorce? She wouldn't fight him. She was too tired to. Instead, she'd simply move on with her life and let her career be enough.

So she said all she could say right now. "Okay. If that's what you want."

She didn't promise she'd be here when he got back, and he didn't ask. While Seb was gone, she had a lot of thinking to do. About what she wanted to do with her life, and if he'd even fit into it after this.

Once that decision was made, there'd be no going back.

So she wished him well and headed on to work, leaving him to pack or do whatever else he needed to do. And Bella would do whatever it was that she needed to do and hope to God that she could figure out what that something was.

And soon.

CHAPTER ONE

AN AMBULANCE SCREECHED to a halt in front of Hospital General de Buenos Aires. It looked like he'd returned to Argentina and the hospital at just the right time, since there were two more parked in the huge entrance of the emergency department. The heat of summer seemed to envelop Sebastián Lopez in a thick layer that made it hard to breathe. Seb stepped up to the open ambulance to see if he could help, only to be met by Gabriel Romero, who was already leaping down and shouting orders to whoever else was inside the vehicle. "Be careful with that neck brace."

Seb peered inside and could only see yellow feathers everywhere. What the hell? It looked like some huge bird had exploded inside the roomy interior of the truck. Then he realized it was a costume. "What have you got?"

Gabriel glanced over and his eyes widened, then the paramedic clapped Seb on the back.

"Well, well, well, welcome back, *porteño!* Or do you not claim Buenos Aires as your home anymore?"

Porteño was the word Argentines used when referring to people who were from the country's capital.

"Very funny." He gave his friend a mock scowl. "I take it your patient has been practicing with one of the Carnival troupes?"

"Yep. And he took one too many steps and fell backward off the stage, landing on his head. He's already got some nasty swelling on the back of his skull."

"Right. Let's get him inside."

Gabriel nodded and pulled the gurney far enough out of the vehicle that the wheels snapped down into place. Hurrying to the emergency entrance, Seb blew a feather away from his mouth as he struggled to keep the long plumes of the costume out of his face. He tried to assess the patient as they went, using his penlight to flick light at each eye. He'd only arrived back in Argentina a few hours ago, and had booked a room in a nearby hotel, not knowing what kind of reception he was going to get from Bella when she found out he was back. He wasn't holding out much hope at this point.

"Pupils are equal and reactive. That's a good…"

He glanced up to make sure he wasn't going to run into anything, and his penlight stopped midair as he spied a familiar face rushing toward them.

"What have we got?" If Bella seemed startled by the costume, she didn't show it. Nor did she show any reaction to him. Or maybe she just hadn't noticed him yet. Or worse, maybe she just didn't *want* to notice him. She hadn't contacted him once since he'd been gone over the last two months, not even to wish him a *Feliz Navidad.* He'd sent her a text and had even tried to call but had gotten no response. Seb was pretty sure that didn't bode well for the state of their relationship. He'd braced himself to receive a divorce petition when he returned. In fact, he'd delayed his flight one week rather than face that possibility, although he'd argued with himself that it was because the little clinic where he'd been working had been overrun with dengue fever cases at the time. But in his heart of hearts, he knew that wasn't why he'd delayed his return.

After all the fertility struggles, he'd decided that if he was never going to be a parent, that was okay. He definitely didn't want to go back down the road he'd been on during that particular journey. Not with her. Not with anyone.

He took a few seconds to glance at her as the paramedics filled her in on the patient. She didn't look any worse for wear. If anything, the slight gauntness she'd developed over their last year of heartache seemed to have melted away. The curves that he'd always loved seemed to have returned full force, despite the shapeless scrubs that didn't reveal much, and her face and cheeks glowed. And her ready smile…it was back.

His leaving had been a good thing for her, evidently. And even though he knew his marriage was very probably over, he was glad that she'd made peace with things in his absence. That she seemed to have rediscovered her sense of self and purpose. He just had no idea where he fit into that. Or *if* he did.

Just then the patient groaned, and Seb leaned in to reassure the man. "Take it easy. You're at the hospital. We're going to take good care of you."

When he glanced up again, Bella had gone dead still, her gaze fixed intently on him, and any color he'd seen in her face just now had disappeared without a trace. Her eyes closed for a long minute before reopening. Then it was as if a switch was flicked back on. Her body reanimated, going about her tasks with the patient as if she'd never stopped. As if his reappearance was nothing more than a minor blip on her horizon that she'd already forgotten about. Indeed, she hadn't even said so much as a hello to him.

Even Gabriel seemed a little uncomfortable at the sudden tension in the room, finishing his report and turning the patient fully over to the hospital staff. As he turned to go, he murmured to Seb, "Give her a little time."

Hadn't he already done that by going to Angola? What else did she need time for? To make the break final? To figure out how to ignore him even more than she already was?

He nodded at his friend as if he understood the words, but in reality his head was spinning with a sense of doom.

They got the patient into a room and transferred him over to a hospital bed, letting the other medical tech take the gurney back out to the emergency vehicle.

She was still avoiding eye contact. Well, to hell with this. He was not going to walk on eggshells around her or anyone. He couldn't do it. Not anymore.

He moved closer to Bella, leaning down to whisper, "We need to talk."

She finally looked at him again and gave a sharp nod. "Once he's stable."

Of course. What else would he have meant? That they just leave the patient and hammer out their personal business in the hospital corridor? No. They were both professionals. They would have to work together, no matter what happened between them.

Unless she was planning on leaving the hospital? A sharp pain went through his midsection at the thought of never seeing her again. Even when he'd been in Africa he'd never once thought of relocating there or making his assignment anything more than an emergency stopgap to assist the staff already on location, who'd been so swamped with patients that they'd struggled to keep up.

Bella was as adept at her job as ever, consulting him briefly as they decided which tests needed to be run. An MRI to rule out traumatic brain or spinal cord injury was at the top of the list.

Once they'd done their physical exam to rule out other problems they could see or feel, the imaging department whisked the patient off to have the scan done. It would take about forty-five minutes before they could get him in and get it finished, so he turned to Bella and found her watching him with wary eyes.

"Do you have time to meet in our office briefly?" he said.

As the joint leads of the ER department, they shared a place to do consults and have meetings with staff. As soon as he said the words, though, he wondered if he was crazy. He and Bella had sometimes made love in his office, whenever her sexiness had particularly gotten to him, back in the early days of their relationship. But it was the only really private place he could think of to talk to her, off the top of his head.

Except she shook her head. "Could we go to the little café around the corner instead?"

She didn't tell him why she preferred going there instead of to the office, but it probably had to do with the same reasons. But it still rankled that she didn't want to be around things that reminded her of happier days. Maybe because those days were long gone, lost in a tidal wave of failed pregnancies and flagging hope.

"Sure. That's fine."

"Let me just tell them where I'll be."

Where *she* would be. Not them. It seemed

she'd already disconnected from him. But maybe it was just as well. Until they could figure out where they stood it was better not to feed the rumor mills with anything that could have people wondering what was going on.

Mainly because he wasn't sure what was going on himself.

So the coffee shop it was.

When she'd seen him with that patient, her heart had skipped a beat. Or maybe it had been five or six, because the shock had quickly given way to other feelings entirely. Hormones. Or maybe it had been that she hadn't been entirely sure he was going to come back at all. That had to be it.

Seb looked as hot standing in a mess of crazy yellow feathers as he did when he'd been emerging from a shower completely naked. The man just did it for her. He always had.

But as she'd learned over the last couple of years, those kinds of feelings weren't always enough. That in trying to drag their love through a minefield of broken dreams, it had emerged tattered and torn, looking very different than it had at the beginning of their relationship. Oh, she definitely still loved him. Still wanted him. But instead of their relationship maturing through the heartbreak they'd shared, it seemed to have crumbled under the strain.

She knew she'd pushed him hard for a baby, but if they'd given up earlier, when he'd wanted to… She had to force her hand not to travel to her growing midsection where three tiny beings were relying on her to keep them safe. That meant no major emotional upheavals. The fact that he hadn't even noticed the change in her body was telling.

Seeing Seb—telling him about the pregnancy—wasn't that going to be one of those upheavals?

It wasn't like she'd purposely kept it from him. She just hadn't wanted to tell him over the phone. Hadn't wanted him to rush home just because of the babies. And if he chose to stay in the marriage for that reason? Oh, *Dios*. She didn't think she could do it. It hit too close to home with her biological father.

He came back from the counter with his café con leche and her herbal tea, which thank God she'd been drinking for years now, so it wouldn't tip him off. Although she was going to tell him. She had to. She'd run out of reasons not to.

She took a sip and sighed as he sat down. He'd added just the right amount of sugar. And somehow the fact that he remembered that made her eyes prick. She blinked and forced back the rush of emotion. This was not how she wanted this meeting to take place. She needed to be strong. Especially now.

"How was your trip?"

"Good." He stared at her for a second or two. "Are you still in the apartment?"

Dios, had he expected her to move out in his absence? Pain slashed through her chest, and she had to force herself not to react. "Yes. I thought it was both of ours."

He sat back in his seat and dragged his fingers through his thick black hair, shoving the unruly locks back off his forehead. It was longer than it had been when he'd left and if anything, it gave him a sexy, rugged air that made her swallow.

"God, Bella, I didn't mean that. I just thought you might have preferred to..." He stopped again. "I wasn't sure if there was even an apartment to go back to anymore or if you'd sublet it to someone else."

"It's still there. *I'm* still there." How could

she tell him, though, that she didn't think it was a good idea for them to live together? At least not until they'd figured things out. She didn't trust herself not to cave in and fall back into old patterns that she was no longer sure were healthy for either of them. It was time to tell him. Time to let him know he was going to be a father. "But there's something I need you to know."

Seb sat in silence, staring at her face as if he didn't want her to say another word. But she had to. He deserved to hear the words so that he could make whatever decision he felt he needed to. So she pushed forward. "I'm pregnant."

"Pregnant." A series of emotions crossed his face. Emotions that she couldn't read. Or maybe she was too afraid of trying to figure them out. "But the last attempt failed."

Even as his words faded away, an awful twist of his mouth gave evidence to what he was thinking. That the babies weren't his. She hurried to correct him. "But it didn't. I assumed when I started spotting that I'd lost the pregnancy, because it was the pattern with the other IVF attempts. And I didn't go to have it checked out right away because of all the stress. I waited until you were gone to try to sort through things."

"So you didn't lose the baby?"

His words were tentative, as if he was afraid that even saying them out loud might jinx everything. She got it. She'd felt the same way when they'd done the ultrasound on her and told her the wonderful news.

"Babies. I didn't lose the babies…plural."

He sat up in his chair. He was shocked. Obviously. But was he also happy? Dismayed? Angry? She could no longer read him the way she'd once been able to.

"You're carrying twins?"

She slowly shook her head, unable to prevent a smile from reaching her lips. "There are three of them."

"*Dios*. Triplets?" His fingers raked through his hair again, but this time there was a desperation to it that caught at her heart. "No. It's not safe."

Safe? What wasn't? "What do you mean?"

"There are risks. Big risks to carrying that many fetuses. Why didn't you tell me, Bella? Surely you could have responded to one of my texts. Before it was too late to…"

Too late to what? Reduce the number? No. That was her decision to make. "I didn't tell you because it didn't feel right doing it over the phone. And I know the risks. I've already told my doctor I'm willing to accept them."

And she was. But was he? Would he turn his back on his own children?

He wouldn't. She knew him well enough to know that. At least she hoped she did. Even if they were through as a couple, she knew Seb would still be an amazing father.

"You made a decision like that without even talking to me?"

This time she did read the dismay in his words. She understood how it probably sounded. That she'd already been cutting him out. And maybe she had been. The way he'd left for Angola had crushed her. She'd wanted to cut him out of her life forever. Had almost convinced herself to go see a lawyer. And then she'd found out she was carrying his children. It shouldn't have made a difference, but it did. In some way that she didn't quite understand.

"How is it any different than when you left for Angola, making that decision without even consulting me?"

He stared at her for a minute before responding. "You're right. I should have discussed it with you first. I'm sorry."

His admission tugged at her heart. But she needed to be careful. The hurt they'd inflicted on each other…the fire they'd walked through didn't vanish with just a few words of regret. It might be something neither of them got over. But this was about more than just the two of them now.

So what did they do? Focus on the babies. And the only way she could think of to help him understand why she was willing to carry multiple fetuses held some emotional risks of its own. But she wanted him to see the reality for himself. To see why the decision to lose one or two of them was untenable for her.

"I—I have an ultrasound scheduled later today if you want to be there. And then I meet with my doctor. You can ask her any questions you want."

There was a moment's hesitation before he said, "Of course I'll be there." He pulled in a deep breath. "I'm in a hotel room at the moment. And I'll stay there until we have time to sit down and decide what to do."

She'd expected him to say that, but still it hurt to hear it. Especially now. Especially after giving him this news. While she'd known he wouldn't sweep her off her feet as he once might have, she had thought he'd show some sign of happiness about the news that she was pregnant. No matter how he felt about her on a personal level. Although maybe he felt it now chained him to her. To the babies.

Give him time, Bella. Time to digest the news.

So maybe it was time to end this meeting and let him do just that.

"Okay. Maybe we can talk more after the ultrasound." She glanced at her watch. "But now I need to get back to the patient. He should be just about done with the MRI at this point."

"And I need to see how much paperwork has piled up in my absence."

They got to their feet, and Seb's eyes traveled over her midsection as if seeing what he'd missed before. When they reached the door to exit the café, he touched her arm, sending a shiver over her. She glanced up at him.

"I'm happy for you, Bella. Truly. I know you've wanted this for such a long time."

He was happy for her. Not for himself. Not for them as a couple.

And that made her heart hurt in a way that it hadn't over the last eight weeks. And she wasn't sure how she would ever get past it.

* * *

Seb sat in a chair in the waiting room of the small IVF clinic that was in an annex of the hospital, feeling completely disconnected from what was happening. He was numb, unsure of how to react to anything. Including the thought that he was going to be a father.

Two other couples were there, and from the little touches and knowing looks that traveled between each of them, they were very much in love. Very much wrapped up in the new adventure of expecting their little ones. And yet here he was. Alone. He'd felt pretty much that way for the last year of their marriage, though, so he should be used to it by now.

He wasn't even sure how they'd gotten to this point. When love had turned to something so unrecognizable that he was no longer sure their marriage was worth fighting for. He'd halfway hoped that she'd made the decision for him, moving out of their apartment and getting on with her life.

In fact, when Bella had first told him she was pregnant, shock had bolted through his system. He'd thought she'd lost the other pregnancy, and since he'd been out of the country...a few soul-sucking thoughts had flown through his head, such as maybe she'd found someone else while he'd been gone. Wasn't that what he'd just hoped for? That she'd get on with her life?

No. Because as soon as the thought had entered his mind, he'd dismissed it. She wouldn't have done that. Not without divorcing him first.

And even the thought of her with another man made his flesh crawl. Whether it was eight weeks from now or eight years. Yet before he'd left Angola, he'd come to accept the fact that they were probably through. That it was only a matter of time before they signed documents cementing that fact.

They said that time healed all wounds, and maybe that was true. But it was tricky when it came to the healing that a couple needed to do to stay together. It seemed, if anything, they'd grown even further apart since he'd been gone. And that was on him. He'd been the one to walk away.

When he'd caught sight of her in that hospital corridor, though, he couldn't deny the rush of relief that had slid through him that she was still there, looking as beautiful as ever. She hadn't disappeared from his life. At least not physically. But emotionally?

The tinkle of a small bell over the door

drove him from his thoughts, and his head turned toward the entrance. Bella. Again, that weird sense of relief swamped him, and it took him a minute to stand up to let her know where he was sitting. It was a signal that had been ingrained in his system, since she tended to run late. The fact that he did it now, when there was no longer any need, made him uneasy. It should be easier to let go—to walk away from something that didn't work—shouldn't it?

Their lives had been consumed by one goal for so long that they hadn't spent the time that was desperately needed to nurture their relationship. And it was damned obvious now that that had been a mistake. A mistake that might just have cost them everything.

"Sorry," she muttered. "I had a patient and couldn't get away."

He glanced down at her middle and saw what he'd missed earlier. The signs of pregnancy were more evident than he'd realized, or maybe the scrubs had just been better at concealing it. Or maybe it was just because he knew the truth. Surely if Gabriel had known, he would have said something to him earlier. And her blouse did a pretty good job of flowing over the swell of her midsection. He forced his eyes back up to her face.

"You're not late. As a matter of fact, you're five minutes early."

"Huh." She said it as if surprised by that information, even glancing down to look at the watch strapped to her wrist. "Well, that's got to be a first."

So much had changed. She had changed. But then again, so had he.

One couple came out—the man dropping a kiss on his partner's head—while another one was called back.

How the hell did he handle being a father when he wasn't even sure he and Bella had a future together? He had no idea. But he'd better figure something out. And soon.

Fifteen minutes of agonizing silence went by before they were called back to the exam room. Liz Everly, their IVF specialist and ob-gyn who'd walked them through the other heartbreaking attempts, was there with a ready smile. She held her hand out to him. "Nice to see you again, Seb. I'm so happy for you both."

He must have mumbled something that made sense because the woman didn't stare at him like he had two heads before she said, "Are you ready to see your babies?"

He swallowed the words he wanted to ask about the likelihood of her carrying this pregnancy to term when so many others had been lost. He wasn't sure he even wanted to see them for fear of that happening. But he'd told Bella he'd be at this appointment, and Seb tried to always keep his word. Even if he might not be able to keep the vows he'd made at their wedding.

One step at a time. You can do this.

But could he? Right now, he wasn't sure.

Liz didn't make her put on a gown. Instead she had Bella hop up on the exam table and lift her top and slide the zipper on her jeans down. Smooth skin came into view. Skin that he'd once loved to kiss. Skin that still made him weak at the knees. Only now that her stomach was exposed to his view, he saw he was right. What used to be a concave surface now sported a definite curve. And her breasts were even fuller than they'd been before he'd left for Africa.

He averted his glance. Everything had become so clinical that they'd both come to view sex as a means to an end. And to look at her now without that hanging over their heads?

It was dangerous. He'd come back from his medical mission with the idea that if she asked him to help her get pregnant again, he was going to suggest a trial separation to see if their goals in life were even compatible anymore. At forty-four, he'd made peace with the fact that he wasn't going to be a father. And yet here he was—about to see babies he hadn't even known existed before today.

She should have told him. A flicker of anger went through him. If he'd known earlier, he could have prepared himself, maybe even wrapped his head around the fact that she was expecting not one but three babies.

Liz squirted a puddle of gel onto Bella's stomach and then picked up the ultrasound wand, running it through the lubricant before getting down to business. There was silence in the room while she searched for the fetuses, and then suddenly a conglomeration of disjointed sounds filled the air. Sounds reminiscent of several metronomes that had all been started at different times. And yet when you tried to separate each out, there was a rhythm to them that was familiar. Comforting, even. A dub-dub, dub-dub that he recognized. But they were so fast.

"Is that…?" His head came up to look at the doctor.

"Yes. Those are their heartbeats. Now let's see if they'll cooperate and let us get a good look at them." She swept the wand around some more, staring at the monitor as a series of shapes moved across the screen.

Then she stopped. "There. There are two of them. The third one must be hiding behind the others."

"I don't see anything." Then he sorted out the shapes and saw them. Realized exactly what he was looking at. A sense of wonder filled his chest, and he felt his own heartbeat increase. *"Dios…"*

His hand automatically started to reach for Bella's before he stopped short. Her silence while he'd been away had made it pretty clear that she hadn't wanted to talk to him. Didn't want to work on their relationship. Maybe she hadn't wanted to tell him about the babies at all. And hell, he could see why. He'd up and left her at a very hard time, right as they'd both thought she was losing the pregnancy. But she'd been ready to ask for another try. He'd seen it in her eyes. And he just hadn't had it in him to cope with any more heartache.

And the heartache of never being with her again?

Not things he should be thinking about at this moment. Especially since Liz was changing the parameters and moving the wand, trying to get a look at the other baby. "Come out, come out, wherever you are." She frowned. "He's pretty well wedged behind the others, but right now I don't see any cause for alarm."

She clicked a couple of areas on the screen, marking measurements of the babies who were out in front. Then she told Bella she could sit up and fasten her clothes before the doctor turned and faced them. Her expression was serious.

Bella's eyes widened. "Is something wrong?"

Even as she asked, Seb felt a surge of panic of his own.

"Not that I can see at the moment. I don't want to dampen the happiness or excitement of seeing your little guys, but I do want to talk to both of you for a minute. Bella, we've already discussed the fact that carrying three babies is tricky, and with your age..."

"I know we have." Bella's voice was soft with a trace of fear. It echoed his own dismay at hearing the words he knew to be true voiced out loud. It was part of the reason he had been done trying. He hadn't wanted to put Bella's life and health on the line in pursuit of something that might never happen. And now that it had, he was quickly realizing just how risky this venture might be.

"I'm going to transfer your care to Dr. Lucas, whose office isn't too far from here. She specializes in high-risk pregnancies."

And there it was. Three words that scared the hell out of him. High. Risk. Pregnancy. But it wasn't just about the babies' lives, anymore, it was about hers as well.

"Are you sure you can't be the one to follow the pregnancy? If I promise to be careful?"

Liz reached out and grabbed hold of her hand, the way Seb had wanted to earlier. "I can't. You need specialized care and constant monitoring. I can't give that to you. But what I can give you is some advice." Her look included Seb this time. "I don't know what is going on between you two, but I felt the tension the second I came into the room. Seb, if you can't be there for Bella, then you need to take a couple of steps back and let her find people who can support her. Physically *and* emotionally."

His wife's teeth bit down on her lip, and she started to say something, but he stepped in.

"It's nothing we can't work out. I'll be there for Bella. Every step of the way." Surely he could do this. At least for the time it took for the babies to be born. He would do whatever it took.

"I'm glad to hear it," Liz said. "You'd be surprised at how many men can't deal with the pressure of finally succeeding with IVF and choose to withdraw emotionally."

Like he'd done when he'd chosen to apply for the position in Africa? Guilt twisted his insides. She was sixteen weeks pregnant, and he'd missed half of it already. But he wasn't going to miss another day of his children's lives.

"You can be sure of one thing. I will protect these babies with my life."

Bella turned to look at him, and there was some strange emotion in her face. And finally she did what he hadn't been able to a few minutes ago: she reached out to squeeze his hand. But she let go again just as quickly. The brief contact sent his world spinning into orbit, and he'd had to clench his teeth to keep his hand from closing around hers to prevent her from pulling away.

And when she pulled away from him for good? Another thing he shouldn't be thinking about right now.

Liz smiled. "Good to hear. Well, I'll let you two get on with your day." She handed Bella a printout of the ultrasound. "And I'll make a note for Dr. Lucas to try and coax that third baby out in the open so we can get a good look at him. I might not be your primary obstetrician anymore, but I'm still your friend. I'll be following your story closely. Call me if either of you have any concerns, okay?"

"I will, Liz. And thank you so much. For everything."

"You are more than welcome. And congratulations again."

With that, the doctor left the room, leaving him alone with Bella.

Before he could talk himself out of it, he said, "I think I should stay in the apartment with you rather than a hotel. I know we haven't decided what to do about our marriage, but Liz made it pretty obvious that you are going to need a lot of support and I meant what I said. I want to be there for our babies—for you—every step of the way. At least until they're born."

The strange look from earlier came over her face again. "I don't want you to feel obligated to live with me just because of the babies, Seb—"

"These are my children, too. I don't want to take any chances."

There was a pause before she responded. "Okay. Like you said, just until they're born. We do have a guest room."

In his rush to support her, he hadn't thought about where he would actually sleep. And he should have been the one to suggest the guest room. But maybe part of him hadn't wanted to make that break. Not quite yet. All of those decisions could wait until the babies were born. Anything to prevent turmoil in her life. In the babies' lives.

"Yes, we do. I'll move my things home from the hotel as soon as we leave here."

"Okay. And Seb, thanks. For everything. I truly mean it."

Although he'd used the word *home* when talking about the apartment, he was no longer sure it held any meaning as far as he was concerned. But for now he would stay there. And do his damnedest not to remember how good things used to be between them in the early days of their marriage. Because those days were long gone, and he wasn't sure there was anything he could do about that. Or if he even wanted to.

CHAPTER TWO

SEB HAD BEEN true to his word and had moved his effects from the hotel last night. And this morning he'd started moving the things he hadn't taken to Angola out of their bedroom while she'd sat in the kitchen and tried to banish her hurt. A hurt that grew with every sound that came from the room down the hall.

She'd been the one to suggest he move into the guest room, but she'd been thinking more about his suitcases from the trip than anything else. But Seb had been pretty quick to move things to the next level by removing all of his possessions from the bedroom they'd used to share. And he'd also made it more than plain that he was mainly there to support the babies. To do that, he had to support her. Talk about emotional turmoil. The very thing that Liz had wanted her to avoid. But the realization that her husband seemed to be more concerned with his future children than he was with her was…gutting. Her mom had probably felt the same way when Bella's biological dad hadn't proposed to her after he'd found out she was pregnant.

Except Seb had proposed all those years ago and hadn't needed a pregnancy to do it. But would he have stayed with her now if the doctor hadn't mentioned her needing help?

Her heart said maybe not. He'd been the one to walk away by taking the Doctors Without Borders gig, even though he had tried to contact her a couple of times during his absence. But there'd been radio silence for the last month. Almost the whole time she'd been trying to process being a mom to triplets.

Again, not his fault.

But at least he hadn't rejected the babies. Then again, her father hadn't rejected her, even though he'd never married her mom. He'd been a great dad, and he'd always said he cared about her mother and had supported her however he could while she was pregnant; he just evidently hadn't loved her enough to take their relationship to the next level. Her mom had ended up marrying someone else when Bella was a year old, who'd also been a great father figure.

She knew this situation was nothing like

the one she'd grown up with. But things between her and Seb had definitely changed over the last year, and while, like her dad, he probably still cared about her, it seemed he didn't care enough to sit down and try to work things out. As evidenced by his quick willingness to leave for Africa…and now to move into the guest room.

The sounds of things being shifted from one room to the other stopped and a minute later, Seb appeared in the doorway. "I got most of it over there. I'll probably just box up what I don't need right now and put it into storage."

Another nail pierced her heart. It was all she could do to nod in agreement. Saying anything in her emotional state right now might make things worse. Or lead to her venting all the pain his absence had engendered over the last couple of months. So instead she said, "It's fine. I need to be at work in an hour, so I'll go get ready if that's okay."

Seb nodded. "I have the day off, so I'll see you when you get home. Unless you want me to drive you to work."

"No." The word came out quickly. Too quickly. She covered by adding, "I think the closer I stick to my normal routine, the better."

They used to drive to work together regularly. Until about a year before he'd left for Africa. Even then the cracks in their relationship had been making themselves known. At the time, they'd blamed it on differing shifts and one or the other of them having to stay longer at the hospital than expected. But looking back, she could see that it was more than that. It had been the beginning of what was probably the end of their relationship.

The triplets were just delaying the inevitable. At least for the next few months.

She couldn't stop herself from grieving what they'd lost. Never in her wildest dreams had she thought they would come to the point where they lived in the same house but might as well have been a thousand miles apart.

Like they had been literally, not even two days ago. Nothing had changed. Except for the ache of seeing him and knowing she couldn't ask him to hold her—to promise her that everything was going to be okay. Because she wasn't sure it would be, no matter what he said.

And if by some horrible chance she lost the pregnancy? Would he just walk away from her?

Who could blame him? She could look back

and see how relentless she'd been in her quest for a baby, even after she realized he was emotionally done with trying. She'd always assumed that once the IVF worked, it would repair whatever had come between them. Instead those cracks had turned into crevasses with her standing on one side and Seb on the other. And he seemed to have no interest in building any bridges.

But then again, she wasn't sure she was interested in that either.

When she got up to walk to the bedroom to get ready for work, he stepped in front of her, making her look up at him. His eyes were soft, and it ignited a flare of hope inside her. "Promise me you'll call if you need anything."

Hope fizzled as quickly as it had come, and pain washed up her gullet. Bella had to swallow the vile-tasting emotion before it robbed her of the ability to think. Because she knew he was talking about the pregnancy and not her as a person. But she managed a smile and glanced up at him and said she would. Then she waited for him to step out of the way and let her by.

He did, but it took a few seconds as he looked at her face as if trying to read something in her expression.

Dios, *please don't let him see the fear and frustration.*

Then he frowned and turned away, walking in the direction of the guest room. She sagged in relief. Or maybe it was in defeat. Right now she couldn't tell one from the other. She only knew that it was going to be a long five months. If they even made it that long under the same roof.

And after the babies were born?

She didn't know. She just didn't know. And that was the hardest thing of all.

Seb heard her moving around the apartment before six in the morning, just as he had for the last few days. She would leave for the hospital soon. Although he hadn't asked for them to have different shifts, it seemed that's how things were lining up right now. Or maybe Bella had asked not to work with him. But that didn't sound like her. She was an incredibly private person. Which was borne out in the fact that no one had yet said anything to him about the babies. He would have expected some congratulations by now. But hell, he was glad for that fact, at least. When he did see her, it seemed she was dressing in a way to deliberately conceal the pregnancy, even though to him it was now pretty obvious. And she was beautiful.

But it was getting more and more uncomfortable knowing she was just two doors down from where he was sleeping. He thought part of that was from only catching glimpses of her now and then. By the time he got home at midnight, she was already in bed asleep.

So far they hadn't hammered out anything firm about her appointments or the delivery, and those were things that should be talked about. Sooner rather than later.

So, finding some jogging pants, he yanked them up his hips and went out into the dark hallway. Why hadn't she turned on any lights? Or was she already gone?

When he turned into the dining room, he crashed against something hard enough to make it tip. Only when he grabbed at it to keep it from falling, it gave a quiet cry and he realized it wasn't some*thing*, but some*one*. Bella.

With one arm around her, he felt the wall for the light switch he knew was there and pushed it, sending light streaming through the room. He blinked, trying to let his eyes adjust to the sudden brightness.

He glanced down at her to find her fully

dressed for the day and pressed tightly against him, a sensation that was so painfully familiar that he had to swallow. Her palms were pressed flat against the bare skin of his chest, and her head was tilted back, her pink lips slightly parted. She looked so much like the girl he'd married ten years ago that in his sleepy state he was having trouble remembering that they weren't that happy couple anymore. Before he could stop himself, he reached up to touch her cheek, his other arm bringing her belly against him.

As if she'd been jolted back to reality, she pushed against him and he released her immediately. "Sorry."

"It's okay. I was trying not to wake you."

"You didn't. I've been awake for a while."

They stood there for a minute or two before he remembered why he'd come out here in the first place. "You don't have to tiptoe around in the mornings, you know."

"You worked late last night, and I was hoping to let you sleep as long as possible."

So different from the days when she hadn't worried about that but had instead woken him up with tiny kisses that had driven him wild with need. The days when they'd made love with a passion that ignited instantly when they'd worked different shifts in the past, coming together whenever they could to stay connected.

There was no longer any need for that, it would seem. In fact, it was as if she was tiptoeing around to avoid seeing him, if anything.

"What time do you work until today?" Was she going to keep the grueling pace of the ER all the way up until she delivered? Liz had emphasized that her pregnancy was high risk. Surely she wouldn't agree with Bella working almost twelve hours a day.

"Five thirty. You?"

"I'm actually taking another day off." He hadn't been planning on that until this very moment. But they'd talked so little since he'd been back that he felt like it was time to get on the same page as far as the pregnancy went.

"You are?" The way she said it showed her surprise. Even though this was the time when new residents had begun working in different areas of the hospital, including in the ER, Seb had never taken personal days. But he knew he wasn't leaving the hospital short. At least not today. He was going to pretend this wasn't a spur-of-the-moment thing.

"I am. I kind of wanted to sit down and talk

about how the next several months are going to go. Have you made an appointment with the specialist yet?"

She blinked a couple of times. "I…um, have. Her office called the other day."

He tensed. She hadn't told him. Or even left him a note to let him know about it. He wanted to be involved, but the question was, was she really going to let him be? "And?"

"I was going to check with you first and see when a good time would be."

A few of his muscles relaxed. Maybe she wasn't going to shut him out completely. "Thank you. Can we meet somewhere after you get off and sit down and talk about that and a few other things? If you're not too tired, that is."

"You know I won't be." This time she said it with a smile.

Bella was the opposite of him in that being in the ER seemed to energize her. She got off duty fully wired and needing time to unwind before she could sleep. And one of the best ways she'd found to do that was to make love. Was she trying to remind him of that fact?

Despite everything, his body immediately reacted to the memory, and he had to grit his teeth and will away the rigidity of the very muscles that would give him away.

He drew a deep careful breath. "Where do you want to meet? Or do you want me to pick you up from the hospital after your shift?"

"No, I think it would be easier for me just to drive to wherever you're thinking. That way I won't have to go back and pick my car up."

That made sense, but he couldn't help but feel that the major reason for the suggestion was to avoid being in close proximity with him as much as possible. Which he got. Even if he didn't completely agree.

How were they going to work things out if they were never together?

They wouldn't. And maybe that was the point she was trying to make. That she didn't want to work anything out with him.

"That's fine." Before he had a chance to think about it he said, "Why don't we meet at the Bosques de Palermo? In the rose garden?"

The famous Buenos Aires park had always been one of their favorite places to walk. In the early days of their romance, they would rent a paddleboat and go out to the middle of the lake and just sit and talk for hours. In between make-out sessions that got hot enough to make them hurry to get somewhere more private. Maybe suggesting that place wasn't the best idea, but to go back and offer up a place with fewer memories was going to sound strange.

When he glanced at her, her teeth were digging into her lip and he thought she might refuse to meet him there. Then she said, "Sure. That sounds okay. It'll take me about twenty minutes to get there, so how about six o'clock, in case I get caught up at the hospital for a little longer."

"Six sounds good." He allowed himself a slight smile. "And thanks for agreeing."

"Of course. We do need to discuss a few things."

His smile disappeared. It might as well have been some kind of business meeting where they hashed out the points of some contract. Well, that's what they'd be doing, wasn't it? Discussing what she expected out of him during this pregnancy.

And afterward?

Well, that was a discussion for another day. And he could tell she was getting antsy…anxious to be on her way. Away from him. "I'll see you there, then."

"Yes. See you." With that, she slid the strap of her small purse over her shoulder and started to turn toward the front door. But not before her eyes slid across his midsection. Only when she was gone and he glanced down did he realize that she'd been looking at his bare chest. The chest she'd rested against just a few minutes ago. And his smile returned. Maybe she wasn't as oblivious to him as she'd seemed. He quickly quashed that idea. It was more likely that she'd felt awkward at his state of undress with his jogging gear slung low on his hips.

Well, at least he'd gotten her to agree to a meeting. Because living like this for the next several months was going to be torture, and it was the exact opposite of what he was supposed to be doing when he'd promised Liz he'd support her during the pregnancy.

So the sooner they figured out what she needed from him, the better he would feel about everything.

At least that was what he hoped. With that, he retrieved his cell phone and called the hospital to request the day off.

The rest of the day passed without incident, but Seb wished he hadn't completely skipped working today. It had left him with too much time to think. And right now thinking was dangerous. As he leaned against one of the pillars of the huge rose arbor, the scents of the flowers surrounding him and offering up a little bit of protection from the scorching sun, he wondered if they should have just met at the apartment instead. Or at least someplace that offered a cool interior. Today was steamy, but at least there were plenty of shady spots in the park like this arbor.

Still, he wondered how much exertion was safe. Then he made a face. The Emergency Department offered her plenty of that on a daily basis.

A few minutes went by, and then he saw her walking toward him. She was now wearing a loose gauzy skirt and a white top with thin straps that bared her shoulders. She'd been wearing scrubs earlier, so she must have changed at the hospital. With her hair pulled high off her neck in a sleek ponytail that bounced with every step she took, she looked cool and collected and…beautiful. Then again, she'd been just as beautiful in her hospital garb. He moved toward her and leaned down to graze his left cheek against hers in the traditional Argentine greeting rather than kissing her mouth. Even so, she flinched at the light contact.

"Sorry, I'm late," she said.

He glanced at his watch and smiled. "I don't think one minute past six constitutes being late. Hard day?"

"Actually? Not really. Just a lot of colds and sniffles. One chest pain case that wound up being indigestion."

Seb remembered the days of the pandemic when a simple cough could signal serious illness. He prayed they would never see something like that again in his lifetime. "You're being careful, I hope."

Her brows shot up. "Of course. Just like I always am."

"Sorry. Habit."

The days of being allowed to worry about her were evidently over. Except some things you couldn't turn off like a switch.

Like his reaction to her this morning?

He pushed that back just as she dismissed his apology murmuring, "Don't worry about it. Do you want to talk here or somewhere different?"

"Do you feel like walking?"

"Yes." She glanced at him, maybe seeing something in his face, because she went on, "I'm fine. Really. How about the bridge?" She motioned to her right where a large white

Grecian-style bridge spanned a narrow area of the lake. From there it was possible to look out over the different zones in the park.

"Sounds good."

He fell into step beside her as they talked about some changes that had happened in the hospital since he'd been gone. They were looking to add a new doctor to the neonatal unit, and she'd heard they had a line on a doctor from Uruguay who was moving to the area with her daughter in the next couple of weeks. "I can't remember her name at the moment, but I've heard only good things about her."

Going up the wide steps that led to the bridge, he started to put his palm on the small of her back like he would have done when things were normal between them, before deciding it wasn't a good idea. "Are they going to interview her for the position?"

"I think so? But I haven't asked specifically." Her hand went to her belly. "It'll be good to have a fully staffed unit when the babies arrive."

They got to the top of the bridge and strolled a few yards before stopping and leaning their arms on the railing. From here it was possible to see the swans cruising down the water, their white plumage shining bright in the sunlight. Off to their right was one of the park's paddleboats. The couple inside was sitting close, then the woman leaned down to scoop up some water and splash it toward her companion. Laughter ensued. When he glanced at Bella, he saw that she was watching them, too, before pulling in an audible breath and blowing it back out.

"So," she said. "What are some good days to meet with the specialist?"

"I'm on three days at the end of this week and off two, yesterday and today being those two."

"It'll probably be next week before we can get in. What's your schedule like then?"

He pulled his phone out to check his calendar. "I'm off the following Thursday and Friday."

"I can make next Friday work. Shall I call her and see if she has an opening on that day?"

"Yes. Probably the sooner we get in the better at this point."

She nodded. "I agree."

He somehow expected her to call once she got back to the apartment, but instead she retrieved her own phone and made a call. "Hi.

This is Isabella Lopez. Dr. Everly referred me to your office."

Bella waited a few seconds, and then he could hear another woman talking. "Oh, yes, Dr. Lopez, she called the office and asked us to get you in as soon as we can. Does this week work?"

Without looking at him, she replied, "Not really. Would you by chance have anything on Friday of next week?"

Seb frowned. If Liz wanted them to get in as soon as possible, wouldn't it be better to go this week? He could certainly ask for more time off. He motioned for her only to have her cover the mouthpiece of the phone and say, "It's okay. Let's just stick with what we talked about."

All he could do was nod. Was this how it was going to be the whole time? He realized they had indeed talked about making the appointment for next week, and she had put the phone on speaker so that he could hear both sides of the conversation, but somehow he felt like he was being shut out. Already.

"Would three o'clock work?"

Bella glanced at him as if seeking his opinion, so he nodded his head and entered the time on his calendar.

The call ended a moment later, and she sighed. "And here we go."

The words were soft, and he wasn't sure if she was talking about the appointment or about their journey through it. Suddenly, she glanced up at him. "Can we rent a boat? I might not get too many more chances before my belly is too big for my legs to paddle. And it looks so cool out there on the lake."

He blinked, unsure if he'd heard correctly. She actually wanted to go out on a boat? With him?

As if sensing his hesitation, she shook her head. "Never mind. I know it's hot and you don't have to—"

"Let's do it." The words came out of their own volition. But he wasn't sorry he'd said them. Maybe this would put them back on a path of being a little more like the friends they'd once been than the strangers they now were.

"Are you sure?"

"I am, as long as you don't think it will tire you too much."

"The exercise will be good for me. I have a feeling I'll need every ounce of strength I can muster for what's coming."

"Okay. But just this once, until we can ask the doctor if it's advisable for the babies."

Something in her face fell, and he hoped he hadn't brought back sad memories of the previous failed attempts at getting pregnant. He hadn't meant to do that, or to alarm her, but he did want her to have the best possible chance of carrying these little ones through to delivery, which would undoubtedly be by cesarean section. He couldn't imagine a doctor who would let her deliver vaginally. Not with her history. Because if something happened to these babies…

It wouldn't. And thinking such thoughts would do neither of them any good.

"We'll take it easy. I promise, Seb."

The words stung, bringing up its own memories of times when he'd been hesitant to make love to her, yet she'd urged him with her hands to come to her with promises that they'd be careful. And while he knew that they had indeed always been careful, with Seb holding himself back and taking care with every gentle thrust, he'd always felt the weight of guilt whenever she'd started bleeding a week or two afterward.

But not this time. Maybe it was good that they were no longer a normal, happy couple.

Because he'd have a hell of a time not giving in to her if she asked him for sex.

That was one thing at least that they didn't have to worry about. Sex.

Even as he thought it, he had to work hard to banish the images that flashed in his mind's eye.

"Let's go. I think they'll be closing up for the night pretty soon."

Crossing the bridge and walking the short distance to the boat rental area, Seb asked for one of the paddleboats and paid for it, then held it while Bella gingerly got on. Then he pushed the vessel offshore and leaped onto the edge of it, hearing her laugh as the boat tipped dangerously under his weight. Hell, the last thing he wanted to do was dump her into the water by accident. Although he could remember a time when he'd done it on purpose. They'd gotten reprimanded by the person on duty that day, but it hadn't mattered. They were young and in love. Right now, Seb felt anything but young. But he was pretty sure he was still in love, although he wasn't going to unpack that too much, since it really wouldn't make much of a difference. Bella was no longer in love with him from the evidence he'd seen. The only reason she was letting him be around her was so that the babies could have a father, which he should probably be grateful for. At least it would give him a few months to get used to the idea of being a father, even if he was no longer a husband in any real sense of the word.

Climbing into his seat, he glanced at her. "Where to?"

"Can we go under the bridge and stop for a few minutes? It's shady there, and we can talk a little more."

Maybe that's why she'd wanted to rent a boat. They were a lot less likely to have people listening to their conversation than if they were sitting on a bench somewhere. Not that anyone here knew them. "Sure. Let's go."

It was as if nothing had changed for a few moments. They'd ridden in these boats countless times over the course of their marriage. They matched each other's pace and steered the vessel with little effort, working as the team they used to be. Before all of the heartache. It made his chest tighten. Why couldn't they have worked so seamlessly together in the harder areas of their relationship? Because relationships were messy even on a good day. Add in IVF and all the stress that went along with it, and it was a recipe for disaster. As they'd both found out.

She bumped her belly with her knee once and laughed. "Yep. I definitely won't be able to do this in a few more weeks. But it feels good to be out here now."

Within two minutes, they'd reached the bridge, and they slowed to a crawl. It was impossible to stay stopped in one place because of the natural current caused by the shifting winds. But they were able to keep to the shady side by correcting course when they reached the edge of the shadows. "Do you still feel okay?"

"I do. I'm fine. Really."

He nodded. "And you trust this specialist?"

"I don't know her personally, but she and Liz are friends, and Liz says she's one of the best in Argentina. And I trust her to tell me the truth. So to answer your question, yes, I trust her. I have to."

He'd trusted Bella to tell him the truth at one time, too. But he saw how much that had changed when he'd first heard she was pregnant and his immediate thought had been that she'd been with someone else—a thought that would never have entered his head a year ago.

Two years ago. So much had changed since then. And not in a good way. Yet she'd never given him any reason to doubt her.

But surely, the same way that they'd so easily changed the boat's direction, they could find some kind of way to stay amicable. To make this whole process as painless as possible. Because he was pretty sure at some point they'd be discussing custody agreements, child support and divorce.

"What kind of instructions were you given? Surely while I was gone, they must have told you what to do—what not to do."

"I'm supposed to walk. A lot. Both for exercise and to keep my joints supple. I'm sure paddle boating would be considered good for both of those reasons."

So was that the reason she'd suggested it? Because it had been recommended? In some small part of himself, he'd hoped maybe it was because this lake held good memories for her. That maybe she wanted to try to get back to where they used to be emotionally. But so far, the conversation was as generic as ever.

"And as far as working goes? How long are you allowed to continue?"

She shrugged. "I think that's probably something I need to ask the specialist. Liz didn't have a whole lot of advice as far as that went."

The swans that had been swimming upstream of them circled back toward them, probably looking for a handout. When they drew even with the boat, she said, "Sorry, *amigos*. We have nothing for you. Not even a cracker." She smiled. "Although a month ago, I was downing them by the box."

"You were sick?"

She glanced at him. "It was normal morning sickness. At the time, though, I thought I'd lost the babies and that it was due to stress and because you'd lef—"

Because he'd left. She didn't need to finish the word for him to know that's what she was talking about. Guilt rose ever higher.

"And when did you find out it wasn't?"

"When I called Liz a couple of weeks later, she told me I needed to come in. That if I'd really lost them, I needed to have a D&C. But when they gave me an ultrasound, they heard what she thought was a baby's heartbeat. Then two. Then three. We were all flabbergasted. And..." She paused, swiping at her eyes. "And so, so happy! Liz and I both fell apart and hugged each other, screaming and crying."

Seb had missed out on all of it. His guilt changed to hurt. “I would have come home if you’d told me, Bella.”

There was a long, pained pause. “You’d left. And I didn’t want to call you back when it was always your dream to be a part of Doctors Without Borders. You evidently stayed extra time, too. So I knew I’d done the right thing in waiting until you came back to tell you.”

He had stayed extra time. But only a few days’ worth. He knew by leaving Argentina in such a hurry, he’d hurt her badly. But he felt like he’d seen the writing on the wall. That she was going to keep pressing for them to try again, even after he’d told her he couldn’t. He hadn’t wanted to ask her for a divorce, but it had been swirling around in his head for a month or two.

And by being too cowardly to stick around and hash things out, he’d evidently missed some pretty spectacular moments.

But he was here now. Right? And divorce was now the furthest thing from his thoughts.

Even if he couldn’t turn things around in their relationship, maybe he could regain her trust. Help her to know he would never knowingly turn his back on his children. So how could he make her believe that?

By being here now? By being the support he'd promised both her and Liz that he would be?

"I'm sorry, Bella. Sorry for leaving like I did. I could say that they were eager to have me on the field, and I wouldn't be lying. But I thought if I stayed in Buenos Aires any longer, it would make it harder on both you and me. I truly believed we needed a break from each other. I still believe that, even though I want to be here for you now—to help however I can."

"That doesn't make sense. How can we take a break and yet not take a break?"

"I think by doing it the way we already are. Having different bedrooms. Different shifts. Different—"

"Did you ask for us to have separate shifts?"

"No, but I don't necessarily think it's a bad thing. It might be easier for both of us that way. It gives us each time to process things."

"But in that case, we really shouldn't be going on extracurricular trips together like this one, should we?"

"I don't think we should avoid each other completely. And every once in a while we do need to talk. To meet for appointments. I think meeting off hospital grounds will help us cope at work when we do have shifts that overlap."

"Whatever is best for the job, right?" Her voice had a tone of bitterness to it.

"That's not what I'm saying. Do you want to work with me every shift? Never be able to get away from me?"

"Well…no, I guess not."

The jab those words gave him was quick and almost painless. Until he realized they were lodged under his skin like a fishhook, and there wasn't much he could do to get them out…or ameliorate the sting.

He cleared his throat. "So, is this better than the alternative?"

She glanced around, and they watched the swans who were gliding away, heading toward a group of people on the shore. "Honestly, it is, Seb. Thanks for suggesting it. I think I needed something like this to help me unwind."

"Then we should do it more often?" So much for all of that stuff he'd just spouted about not spending a lot of time together.

"Yes. We should." She laid her hand on her stomach. "At least until I can no longer fit in the boat." She gave him a rueful grin.

"Then we'll find another activity to take its place."

Too late he realized how she could take those words. Especially when her cheeks turned pink. Or was that from the warmth of the day? Either way, it was probably better to call a halt to this outing before she really did become overheated. Or before he did.

As if she knew what he'd been about to say, she beat him to the punch. "Are you ready to go in? I think the vendor is motioning all the boats to move toward shore."

He thought she was just saying that until his glance turned toward the rental place and he saw that the man was indeed waving at them. Actually, it looked like they were the only ones still out on the lake.

So it was time to end this field trip. He had to agree with her. It had been nice. Maybe a little too nice. But in the face of the alternative, he would take it and run with it. For as long as she would let him. Even though it might be harder when it all came to an end.

CHAPTER THREE

THE APARTMENT WAS quiet when Bella left a few days later. This pattern of getting up early and being super quiet so she could leave before he woke up was starting to wear on her, even though he'd told her not to bother. But it was easier this way. Especially after their little trip to the Bosques de Palermo. It had been so reminiscent of the old days that when she spotted him leaning against that arbor looking like a Greek statue that had come to life, she'd had to restrain her quivering mouth. Her emotions had come roaring back from the abyss and were crying out for her to go to him and put her arms around him. To lean her head against his chest and breathe in his scent. But she couldn't. And the urge to turn around and run had never been so strong. Besides, there was nowhere to go. Even if they eventually divorced, she was still going to have to see him every day—work with him on some of the same cases.

Unless she moved to another city. But even then, it wouldn't be an answer. She didn't intend to keep the babies from him—even if she could, she didn't want to—and so she would still have to see that rugged, beautiful face of his fairly often. Maybe she shouldn't have sent plea after plea up to *Dios* for the in vitro to work this time. But even the thought of something happening to the babies at this late stage filled her with fear.

No. She was going to have to be around him. And honestly, the more little side trips they took and the more he was involved in this part of the pregnancy, the better. She'd get used to it, right? Being near him without him being a part of her life anymore? Even the thought of it made her heart cramp. He'd talked about them needing their space. And in some ways she agreed with him.

She just wasn't sure she would ever become immune to him, no matter how much space there was between them.

Realizing she'd been sitting there deep in thought for the last fifteen minutes, she started the car and shifted it into reverse before she remembered that she'd set her lanyard on the kitchen counter when she went to drink a second glass of milk.

Maldición! She couldn't go through her day without it. She needed it for a lot of tasks at the hospital including the computer system and the medicine cabinets. She was going to have to go back into the apartment just as quietly as she'd left it. Sighing and hoping the rest of her day didn't follow this negative trajectory, she turned off the car and pocketed the keys. Going back up the elevator, she unlocked the door and opened it. But expecting to be met with a dark space, she was shocked when she opened the door to find the lights glaring, blinding her for an instant. She was pretty sure she hadn't switched anything on, which meant…

Seb was awake somewhere in the apartment. She blinked a couple of times before her eyes adjusted. She tried to creep toward the kitchen, hoping to retrieve the lanyard before he appeared from the guest room. Quietly picking her way toward the kitchen, she stopped midstride with the light from hallway flicked on. Her eyes shot toward the space and realized Seb was coming out of the bathroom. And he was naked, water streaming down and following the contours of his body.

And those contours were heavenly. Just like a Greek statue.

She swallowed hard, freezing in place.

He hadn't seen her yet, his hands sliding through his hair and ruffling it, sending water droplets flying in all directions.

At one time, this would have driven her wild, but in a completely different way than it was right now. She would have been irritated that he was dripping water all over their expensive hardwood floors. Seb, however, would just smile that secretive smile of his and it would change everything in a flash.

She winced, realizing she'd made some kind of squeaked sound that caused Seb's head to turn her way. Her eyes widened in horror.

So much for collecting her keys and getting back out before he got up.

Her nipples tightened as she stood there and stared, a wave of need going through her that was more powerful than anything she'd felt in a long time. She forced herself to stay right where she was, telling herself if she walked toward him things were going to get messier than they already were. Not to mention he could very well reject her.

But hell, while she could stand there rooted

in place, she couldn't make her eyes follow suit, and they were busy sliding over every wet inch of his body. Until she reached…

And like a master puppeteer pulling a string, it started to rise.

That made her move. Fast. But not toward him. She crossed the hallway and ducked through the door into the kitchen. "Sorry," she called. "I forgot my lanyard."

When she turned back toward the door, her errant key card in her hand, there he was. Again.

"Sorry," he murmured with a wry smile, still naked. "I forgot my towel."

She blinked, keeping her eyes averted this time.

Was he trying to torment her? He walked past her and into the laundry room, coming back a few seconds later with a towel slung around his narrow hips. But there was still a telltale sign of his reaction to her stares that she could see even through the terry cloth fabric.

She hauled her lanyard around her neck, gripping it tight when she found herself hoping the edge of that towel would come untucked. How long had it been since she'd been able to look at him for pure enjoyment's sake?

A long time. But he was no longer hers to do that with, and if he'd accidentally come into the bathroom and stared at her like that, she probably would have yelled for him to get the hell out of there. But he hadn't.

And from what she'd just seen…

The man wasn't totally immune to her. She didn't know yet how she felt about that.

If anything, it was going to make it harder to make rational decisions. To not let her emotions get all caught up in the memories—in the sights and scents—of what they'd once meant to each other.

But she had to figure it out somehow, or she was going to be doomed to fall back in love with him.

And that would be a disaster, right?

He'd made it pretty clear that he was here only to support her because she was carrying his children, not because he wanted to go back to being married in the real sense of the word.

And her reaction to him? Hormones. It had to be. Hadn't she read that women started feeling all kinds of crazy things as they went into their second trimester? And coming up on seventeen weeks, she was definitely there.

"There are towels in the linen closet. You

didn't have to go all the way to the laundry room for one."

His smile widened in a wicked way she remembered so well before he said, "I know."

That made her run for the hills before she could cut apart and analyze exactly what he meant by that. Because she was afraid if she didn't get out now, she might not leave at all.

Seb hadn't meant to make her uncomfortable. But hell if she hadn't stared at him like she'd never seen him before. And it had been enough to make him want what he couldn't have. But, damn it, to parade himself naked in front of her like that? It reeked of desperation, and he'd sworn to himself multiple times, as he lay there at night unable to sleep because he knew she was just a few steps away, that he wasn't here for sex or intimacy or anything that went along with it. He was here because her doctor thought she needed the extra support. Plus he hadn't found another place to live. Not yet. But maybe it was time to start doing that.

Their current apartment only had two bedrooms, and the guest room was pretty small, as his shin could attest after being knocked against the wooden footboard of the bed a couple of times now. And with triplets? It would seem even smaller. But right now there was literally not another bedroom he could sleep in besides the one he was in. And to get three cribs in that tiny space in addition to the bed that was already in there? It was probably impossible without somehow stacking them bunk bed–style against the wall—not the best idea.

The thought of leaving this place and going their separate ways, though? That was a hard pill to swallow. But it was bound to happen in a few quick weeks. Her pregnancy suddenly seemed far too short. For him, at least. He doubted any other human being on the planet had ever thought that, but right now, the birth of their babies probably spelled the end of their relationship, and that was a kick in the gut.

To deal with it, he got dressed and decided that rather than fixing breakfast in the large kitchen, he would go out to a nearby café and get something. He could get to work early today and do some paperwork in their office. With that, he closed and locked the apartment and headed to the hospital.

Even hours after he arrived, however, the memory of her parted lips as she'd stared at him plagued him, making it almost impossible to concentrate. But he needed to. And in actuality, just because she'd had a physical reaction to him didn't mean they would reconcile. For the very same reason that him having his own very visible reaction to her didn't change the fact that things were still not good between them. And they might never be again.

Oh, they were on the surface, in how they were civil to each other. But underneath it was a whole different ball game. She had to be angry with him because of the last time they were together when he'd refused to try IVF again. And the fact that she was carrying this pregnancy was proof that she might have been right, and him saying no might have deprived her of ever having biological children.

He'd been wrong. Only at the time, he'd been convinced he was doing the right thing. Not just for him, but for her. To save her from the heartbreak she'd experienced time after time during her fertility treatments.

Did that mean that what might seem like the right decision at any given moment would later on turn out to be the wrong one?

Like his vague hope that they might work things out? Ten years from now, would he laugh at how wrong he'd been and how ludicrous the idea of them still being together was?

Damn. Coming in to work had not helped at all. Just the opposite, in fact, because Seb knew that Bella was out there somewhere, probably run off her feet while he sat in a nice cool…calm…office.

Calm? Maybe in the physical sense. But his brain was running at top speed trying to figure out a solution that would work for both of them and coming up with absolutely…nothing.

Tossing his pen onto his desk, he stood and stretched his back. He might as well just head out to the floor. Maybe physical work would keep his thoughts at bay, or at least give him something else to concentrate on. If they were working on different patients they would barely see each other. Which was what they both wanted.

They were both head of the department, and by him leaving for Africa, she'd had to shoulder a lot of the day-to-day running of the ER, something he hadn't really thought about when he'd left.

He wasn't due in for his shift for another four hours, so his sudden appearance made heads turn, although it really shouldn't. Seb had been known to work long hours. But the one person he didn't see was Bella.

And he wasn't going to ask.

He headed to the desk to see which patient was next, only to run into Gabriel, who looked like he was signing paperwork for one of his runs. The EMT turned and smiled.

"Hi, *porteño*. Long time no see."

Seb laughed. "Yes, it's been almost a week. We need to go out for a *cerveza* and catch up." Then he got serious. "How's life been treating you?"

"I can't complain." He grinned. "Well, I could, but it wouldn't do any good. You?"

He wasn't quite sure how to answer that, only to have Gabriel save him by holding up a hand. "Never mind. I probably don't want to know."

"Even *I* probably don't want to know."

Bella appeared. And to his relief she didn't look run off her feet. She looked as fresh as she had back at the apartment. "Don't want to know what? Something about the patient you brought in?"

For once, Gabriel looked uneasy, shifting from foot to foot. "No. Just stuff about Seb's trip."

Bella's head tilted as if she wasn't sure if she should believe him. But if she was going to ask, she didn't get a chance because Gabriel said something about his partner waiting for him in the truck and needing to get back to it.

He threw a parting shot back at Seb, though. "And, *porteño*, I'm holding you to that *cerveza*. Let's make it sooner rather than later, okay?"

His wife's quizzical look wasn't lost on Seb, but she didn't ask this time. Maybe, like him, she wasn't sure she wanted to know.

Then she said, "Did you tell him?"

"Tell him what?"

"About the pregnancy."

Shock held him still for a minute. "He doesn't know?" He'd thought as much, but had wondered if he was right. She was in her second trimester and was definitely starting to show. He was really surprised his friend hadn't guessed.

"I—I haven't told anyone. I thought if I did that it might…"

Her words trailed off, and suddenly he knew why she'd kept it a secret. A thread of anger replaced what had happened this morning. "You thought it might get back to me while I was in Africa, is that it?"

"I didn't want you to hear about it that way."

"Are you sure? Because it's starting to feel like you didn't want me to hear about it at all." He sucked in a deep breath. "What if I'd delayed coming back even longer, Belle? What if it had been four or five more months? Would you have let me know about it then? Or would I have come back to find out that I had three children I didn't even know about? Do you know what I thought when I came back and you finally told me?"

"I can probably guess."

"Hell, I thought you'd miscarried when I left. So when you told me you were pregnant, my first thought was that you'd been with someone else."

Her face went deadly pale, and she glanced around. "Not here!"

He realized his voice had risen enough with that last sentence that a couple of nurses were looking at them. "Let's go around the corner."

He stalked toward a hallway that contained linens and supplies and tended to be quieter than some of the main areas.

When she stopped in front of him, her face was stricken. "You seriously thought I would cheat on you?"

Maldición! He shouldn't have said anything,

but especially not that. He shouldn't have let his anger and resentment cause him to lash out at her. Especially not in her state. Remembering what Liz had said about keeping her stress as low as possible, he touched her arm. "It was only for a split second, then I realized you wouldn't have. Just like I wouldn't have. But our relationship was such a damn mess and I was hurt—I felt you'd kept something important from me. That you would have kept the babies from me altogether if you could figure out how to."

"No, I would never do that to you. You have to believe me. I just didn't want you to hear about it by phone or text. Or worse, by the hospital's rumor mill. When you were later coming back than you said you'd be, I decided I'd tell you if there was another delay." Her teeth came down on her lower lip. "I'm sorry I pressed you so hard for so long to keep trying."

He slid his arm around her waist and gave her a light squeeze. "The only important thing right now are the babies, okay? Let's concentrate on them."

She stiffened for a second, then pulled away, her eyes avoiding his. "Yes. You're right. They're the only things that are important. And we might as well start letting people know that they exist, because it's going to come out soon enough." She touched her belly. "But as for us, let's stick to discussing them rather than personal stuff between us from now on."

In other words, the subject of where they stood as a couple was off the table. Maybe because she'd already come to a conclusion where that was concerned, and from her words the news wasn't what he wanted to hear. But even if he didn't want to hear it, he needed to respect what she was saying and try to remember that this was no longer about them. They were only together because of the babies. And the sooner he got that through his thick skull, the sooner he could figure out where to go and what to do after the babies were born and his "services" were no longer needed.

A nurse appeared around the corner. "Hey, guys? We could use your help."

He'd forgotten for a second that Bella was supposed to be on duty. "What's up?"

"We've got three patients who've all overdosed on something. We need some extra hands."

They rushed back down the hallway, all

thoughts of relationships and talking forgotten as they came on a frenetic scene. One patient was on the floor of the waiting room seizing while a nurse and one of their interns leaned over him trying to get his vitals. Another guy was unresponsive on the ground nearby. A third guy, who'd evidently driven his car partway through the doors of the emergency room, cracking the glass of one of them, had exited his car and was drunkenly ambling toward them. Bloody foam dribbled from the sides of his mouth, and his teeth gnashed in a way that Seb had only seen in horror movies. A woman was crying inside the car. Bella started to hurry toward the man, who was slowly moving in their direction but Seb grabbed her arm, a sudden fear going through him. "Can you go talk to the person in the car? See if she knows what they took? I'm going to get security down here before someone gets hurt."

Bella's brows drew together for a second. "I can handle myself, Seb. I don't need you to step in and—"

"It's not a matter of handling yourself. We don't know what he took and if fentanyl is involved…"

"Oh, God." As if realizing the ramifications of being exposed to some of the crazy drugs people took nowadays, she headed toward the car instead.

As if already alerted, two security officers came down, already gloved and masked, while Seb hurried to do the same. Together, they managed to get the guy on a gurney and strapped down so he couldn't hurt anyone.

His pupils were pinpoints, and when Seb checked with the doctors treating the other patients, they reported the same thing.

Bella came back. "They all injected heroin. The girl didn't take any, but she said there've been reports of it being laced with something. Other people have gotten sick as well."

Sure enough, Seb found tracks on the man's arms. "Let's get some naloxone down here."

Unfortunately, as in large cities all over the world, illegal drugs were a problem that seemed never-ending. Even as he thought it, the police were taking the woman out of the car and putting handcuffs on her. Those drugs affected everyone around the users, including people who hadn't taken it. He had no idea if she was a girlfriend or someone's sister or friend, but she'd just witnessed the horrors that went along with overdoses. Hopefully it would be enough to scare her into wanting nothing to do with it or with those who were unwilling to get help with their addictions.

They dosed the seizing patient with the reversal agent first to see if it had any effect. It did, almost immediately. They followed with the other two patients and waited until it took effect. By then there were four more police officers in the ER, waiting on reports.

Bella went over and talked to them, letting them know everything that they knew so far. Seb had no doubt that once the crisis was over and the patients were stable, each of them was going to pay a hard price for what they'd done.

They'd almost paid with their lives, had been very lucky that the man who'd gotten out of the drivers' seat hadn't crashed into something and killed them all. And Bella walking toward that man had made his stomach twist in a way that had made him act without thinking. He was pretty sure he was going to pay for that later himself.

The police accompanied the patients to the rooms, handcuffs at the ready. Seb gave instructions on watching them to make sure the Narcan kept them stable enough to release into police custody.

As soon as things were under control, everyone breathed a sigh of relief. A tow truck came out and pulled the car from the entryway, and maintenance people came to see about getting the cracked window replaced.

And when he turned around, he knew for certain he was in big trouble.

Bella was standing there, arms crossed. "Listen. I know you were worried, but you do need to know that I would not have put myself in danger. I wasn't going to try to tackle him to the ground or anything."

"I know. It's just that in your condition—"

"Exactly what condition is that?" Her voice was tight with anger.

Seb was confused. He was pretty sure she knew what he was referring to. "Do you think Liz would want you trying to control a man hyped up on *Dios* knows what? A man who's also three times your size?"

"I told you I wasn't going to try to tackle him or restrain him on my own. But you have to trust me to do my job. To know when to step in and when to step back and let security take the lead. We've been trained in this. Hell, Seb, we've trained med students for years on crisis intervention."

He was right; he was going to pay. But looking at it from her side, she was the one who was actually right. "I know that. I was just worried about..." He shrugged. "I was worried about the babies."

"Maybe you should let me worry about them, since I'm the one carrying them."

Continuing this conversation wasn't going to do either one of them any good and was just going to create the very thing Liz said she was supposed to avoid: stress. Time to wave the white flag.

"You're right. I overstepped, and I'm sorry. It won't happen again."

She gave a curt nod. "Make sure it doesn't. Now I'm going to go and make sure the patients—all of them—are ready to be released."

With that, she stalked off. Away from the conversation. And away from him.

The only important things were the babies.

Seb's words, as well as his actions during the interactions with their overdose patients, had put a face on what she feared most. That their relationship was dead, and the only thing left from it were the tiny beings they had created together. Actually, they hadn't even done that. Their babies hadn't been the product of them coming together in love, they'd been created in a test tube and then inserted inside her. They'd each just contributed their genetic material. And it seemed that Seb wasn't willing to contribute anything more.

Not fair, Bella. He'd made it clear that he wanted to have a role in raising his children. And he'd honestly been worried about her putting herself in harm's way. So it was obvious he wasn't leaving her completely alone. She'd see him periodically. And he'd worry about the kids. It would be a heaven and a hell of her own making.

She'd never asked her mother point-blank if she'd been in love with her biological father. If it had devastated her to find out that he hadn't wanted to be with her in a more permanent way. And it was something she would never ask.

Her mom had gotten through that pain somehow, and so would Bella.

The same way she'd gotten through two months of Seb's absence. That had been unbearably hard. Especially when she'd found out she was carrying triplets. The fantasy of him coming home and sweeping her off her feet and professing his continued undying love had come and gone. He'd done neither of those things. Any feelings he'd had for her had probably been crushed by her desperate search for the holy grail of having a baby.

She'd seen it in his face during their last discussion before he'd left for Africa.

Unfortunately for her, she didn't have to worry about falling back in love with him. She already knew she was still crazy about him. But she was also coming to realize that wasn't enough. Love couldn't be one-sided and survive. If he stayed in the relationship just because of the babies, she would soon grow to resent him. And he would resent her if she pressed him for more. So it was better to let him go now.

He'd still been in the ER when she finished with their patients. She walked past him, telling him she needed to get something. And she had. She'd needed to pull her dignity back around her like a cloak and use it to hold back any of the softer feelings she had toward him. How pitiful would it be if he realized she still loved him?

She wouldn't be able to bear it. So he couldn't know. And while she'd told him there was no longer a reason to keep the pregnancy a secret, that didn't hold true for her feelings. They needed to stay tucked deep inside her where he would never guess they existed. She leaned against a wall and tried to catch her breath.

Finally regaining her composure, she headed

back out onto the floor. Where she would probably see Seb again. But when she emerged, the ER was oddly quiet. There were no pressing emergencies. She glanced at her watch. It was noon. Maybe potential patients were eating their lunch before heading in. But whatever it was, she was going to embrace it, just liked she hoped she could embrace her new reality: that of a single mother. At least once the babies were born, their time would be divvied up between two separate households. Because there was no way she and Seb were going to live in the same house once the triplets came. She wouldn't be able to bear it, and she doubted Seb would want that either. He was probably anxious to get on with the next phase of his life. The one where his children were the only important things and where Bella was relegated to the past.

It was how it needed to be. But that didn't mean it was how she wanted it to be.

She knew you didn't always get what you wanted. So she would get the next best thing. Lunch. And she'd do her best to convince herself that it was the only thing she wanted.

CHAPTER FOUR

THE FRIDAY OF their appointment came, and a strange sense of quiet resignation seemed to have arisen between them. He convinced himself that it was better than the uneasy truce they'd had, where one careless word could send them back to their own corners to wait for the next verbal skirmish. The week had been hard. Seb had met Gabriel for beers just like he'd promised and had told him about the triplets and that despite the joy he felt about them, he wasn't sure he and Bella would stay together after they were born. The fact that that his friend wasn't as surprised about that as he was about the babies said it all. He doubted that Gabriel would be an isolated case. Did everyone in the hospital know how bad it had gotten between them?

He was getting ready to meet Bella for her appointment with the specialist when he was stopped in the hallway by a colleague. "Hey, congratulations, Seb! I heard about the babies. How great that you and Isabella were able to work out your differences. It gives the rest of us married people who are having some issues hope."

Damn. So he was right. People did know about their problems. Had their situation looked that hopeless? And what was he even supposed to say to that? His private life was really no one's business, but he also didn't want to lie and say that things were great when they were anything but. But he could try to work out a canned response later on. So for now he just stuck to saying, "Thanks," and left it at that.

Especially since Bella came around the corner, obviously looking for him. Fortunately the other doctor didn't stick around and chitchat some more; he simply smiled and continued on his way.

"Are you ready?" she asked.

"Yep. Let's take my car."

She hitched her purse further up her shoulder. But unlike when they'd driven separately to the park, this time she didn't argue. "Sounds good. You know where it is?"

"I do. I pulled it up on my phone. It's about

a fifteen-minute drive, and it's near the Rio de la Plata."

The rich sediment at the bottom of the famous river was often churned up as the water flowed into the Atlantic Ocean, giving portions of it a brown appearance. But its biodiversity was impressive, and it played an important part in the area's ecosystem.

"Liz said it's a really nice clinic, and of course the babies will still be delivered at our facility, since it's also one of the hospital's clinics."

They got into Seb's vehicle, and he carefully backed out of the hospital parking lot, which tended to be tricky with his larger SUV.

"Wouldn't it be easier to have a car the size of mine?"

He threw her a glance. "You used to love this vehicle. And I'm not sure three car seats will even fit in yours."

"I do still love this car. And you're right. I just…" She shrugged. "I'm just realizing how many things are going to change once these kiddos are born."

Including their living situation. She hadn't spelled it out, but then again, she didn't need to. He glanced at her. "Things can't always stay the way they were."

There was silence in the car for a few awkward minutes before she murmured, "No, I guess they can't. Life moves forward, even when it's not what we planned for."

The roads were crowded, even though it wasn't rush hour yet. But then Buenos Aires was a huge tourist destination. So the traffic wasn't solely due to the city's residents, but also rental cars and buses and the ubiquitous motorcycles that tended to dart in and out of traffic whenever they felt like it. Despite the fast pace of the cars around him, Seb was painfully aware that he was carrying precious cargo. Not just the babies, but Bella as well. He was not going to take any risks that he didn't have to take.

Like leaving the country and letting her face things alone?

"I think your phone is telling you to turn left at the next corner."

"Thanks." He'd been so busy concentrating on the cars around him that he'd almost missed the GPS's instructions.

He put on his signal and edged over just in time to make the turn. He only realized how hard he was gripping the steering wheel when Bella's knee bumped his. "Do you want me to help navigate?"

It was something they'd once done, with her looking at the phone's digital map and letting him know if there was a turn coming up and how far away it was.

"That would be great. Thanks." It would be a lot like old times. Happier times.

He gave a mental sigh and listened as she gave instructions that were off in the distance, even as the computerized voice let them know when they were close to the turn. Within ten minutes they'd arrived at their destination: a large white house that had evidently been converted into a specialized maternity center that contained state-of-the-art equipment.

Finding a parking space near the back, they got out, and Seb was struck by the pristine landscaping that the clinic had done. A small area of green grass was flanked by a walkway from the parking area and another path that led the way to the front door. Two potted bougainvillea stood on either side of the entryway, their crimson blooms striking against the building's whitewashed facade. There was patio on one side, over which stretched a pergola that provided some relief from the summer heat.

Entering the lobby, they found a sign directing them to check in at one of the windows to the left. They went over and waited behind another couple. The woman was obviously getting close to term and was telling her partner that she'd be glad when she could see her feet again. Out of the corner of his eye he watched as Bella's head bent as if looking at her own feet.

She was gorgeous, and he had no doubt she'd be just as gorgeous when she, too, had trouble seeing past her stomach.

He let her do the talking when they got to the window. And when they looked past her to him, she introduced him as her husband.

It made something in his chest tighten. How many more of those introductions would he get? He knew the day would come when the prefix "ex" would be placed in front of that word. When he would no longer be her husband, but just someone from her past. Someone she hadn't wanted to stay connected to any longer.

But for right now, the word was still valid. And he was glad. More glad than he probably should be.

"If you'll just have a seat, we'll call you both back in a few minutes."

Bella thanked them, and he let her lead them to a seating area of her choosing. He had to smile when she picked a row in the back. She never had liked sitting up front, even in medical school. She preferred to sit back and observe, claiming she could pay just as much attention back there as she could up front—where she felt conspicuous.

They'd just barely settled into their seats when a door at the front of the room opened up and her name was called. "Yikes," she whispered. "I hope Liz didn't try to get us special treatment."

He understood her reservations, but triplets were probably something they didn't deal with on a daily basis. They went through to the back and were ushered to a door on the right side of a long hallway. Once inside, a nurse came in and took her weight and blood pressure and had her lie down on the table so they could get a measurement of her belly.

"Everything looks good. Dr. Lucas will be with you in just a few minutes to do a more in-depth exam."

True to her word, there was soon a knock at the door, and an older lady came into the room. She had long wavy gray hair that she wore loose around her shoulders. "You must be Mr. and Mrs. Lopez. I'm Jessica Lucas." She settled on a stool and turned to face them.

"So you're expecting triplets through IVF treatments. Were three embryos implanted?"

Bella nodded her head. "Yes. Dr. Everly knew I'd lost several pregnancies, and she hoped at least one would take this time. Instead they all did."

"And you chose not to undergo a reduction procedure?"

Seb tensed. He'd wondered about the exact same thing.

"No. I thought this might be my only chance to have children, so I'm opting to carry them all to term. Or at least I hope to."

"I understand. It will make it a little trickier for us, but we've delivered several other triplets, and Dr. Everly has a good track record for healthy embryos." She smiled and reached over to pat Bella's hand. Then she looked at both of them. "Do you have names picked out yet?"

"N-no." Bella's voice was soft. "I haven't even gotten that far yet. Maybe I'm afraid that I'll jinx things. I just worry that..."

"Hey. Let me do the worrying, okay? If there's cause for concern, I promise I'll tell you, okay?"

Bella visibly relaxed. "Thanks, Dr. Lucas."

"Call me Jessica, please."

Dr. Lucas stood, swooshing her thick strands of hair behind her shoulders in a gesture that made him smile. She would fit in with the counterculture movement that had started in El Bolsón over on the southwestern side of Argentina. He'd taken a trip over there in his teens and had been fascinated by the village, where self-sufficiency was the name of the game and where freedom of expression was valued above most other things.

"Let's get this show on the road. I know you just had an ultrasound last week—I have those scans from Dr. Everly, but I want to do our own as a baseline, although we're a little late to the game. She also said she had a hard time seeing one of the triplets. If you'll hop up on the table and pull up your shirt and slide the waistband of your skirt low on your hips, we'll get things started."

Seb stood to help her onto the table, also lending a hand and tugging the gauzy skirt low on her hips. He had done it so many times in the past and had never thought twice about it, but now there was an intimacy to the act that made him hyperaware of her. His fingers lingered for a second on softness of her skin. Her belly seemed even more rounded this week than it had been last week. Her breasts were also fuller. He'd never gotten to see any of these changes in their previous attempts, as the pregnancies hadn't held long enough to make a difference in her appearance.

It suddenly made things seem very real to him. So real that yet again he was incredibly uneasy that something might happen. That they might lose the babies that had been growing inside of her for seventeen weeks.

"Damn machine. I can never get it to… There!"

Bella's eyes met his, and her lips twitched, then as if she couldn't contain herself, she giggled. He smiled back at her in return, lifting his brows the way he used to, letting her know that he knew exactly what she was thinking.

He did?

Hell, he hadn't felt that way in a very long time. And he needed to be careful now. He couldn't let one light moment fool him into thinking things between them were better. They weren't. The fact that he'd abandoned her to go to Africa was starting to weigh even heavier on his mind. He should have been here for her. Should have seen her through whatever was coming. But he'd been afraid if he had that he might end up making a decision that he hadn't quite been ready to make.

That he still didn't want to make. Even though he knew it was probably coming anyway. They were still staring at each other. Still smiling.

He heard the sound of something being rolled toward them, and he broke eye contact so he could move away and let the specialist put the machine where she wanted it. "Why don't you go to the other side of the bed, where you can see the screen. Oh, and let me know when you come up with names, so we can label them. For now we'll just assign letters to them."

Seb did as she asked and walked around the head of the bed and wound up on Bella's right side. She reached for his hand, and he took it as Jessica put the transponder on her belly and started moving it around, staring at the screen.

Again, it was something they'd done time and time again, held hands as they awaited the specialist's verdict. It was like muscle memory. Something that had been engraved into their DNA. Kind of like when he automatically felt for her in the middle of the night only to find the bed empty of anyone but him. Only the bed he now slept in was no longer "their" bed. It was for some nameless, faceless guest. Yet he'd now become that amorphous person. Just some temporary human who would pass through her life periodically.

Like when he came to pick up the kids on agreed custody days? His fingers tightened on hers as if already unwilling to let her go.

His attention jerked back to the screen, his mind on high alert, when Jessica made a slight hmphing noise.

"What is it?" Bella's voice was shaky.

He threaded his fingers through hers, laying his other hand over them for added support.

"Nothing. I'm just trying to coax that third little guy out from behind his or her sibling. I can see the baby's little bottom—" she pointed to the screen "—but his chest and head are tucked behind the other baby." She made another noise. "It's okay. We have time." The words were soft, as if she were talking to herself.

Time for what?

Just like last week, he heard the heartbeats and this time, he could make out the babies' forms without any help from the doctor. He watched as Jessica labeled the babies with *A*, *B* and *C* and put little symbols at the head and bottom of each of them, except for baby *C*, who was still not cooperating.

"Can you tell the gender of them yet?" Bella's question came out of nowhere.

Jessica stopped and looked at her. "I'd have a more accurate guess for you next week or the week after that. I would like you to come back in. Hopefully by then we'll get Baby Lopez number three to come out and wave at us. Right now, besides being behind baby *B*, he or she is facing towards the back, which also makes it a little more challenging to see any parts."

Bella wanted to know the gender of the babies ahead of time? It was something else they hadn't really talked about, having never gotten that far in the process. And honestly, he was good either way, although having an *A*, *B* and *C* stuck on that screen bothered him in a way he didn't understand. Maybe they should start playing the name game.

Or would Bella prefer to do that on her own? He was hyperaware of her hand tucked in his. Of her palm brushing across the skin of his.

Hell, he hoped not. When he said he wanted to be a part of their children's lives, he meant it. He was interested in every aspect of it.

Surely they could work together on that, the same way his work colleagues collaborated to make decisions about the ER. The way he and Bella would have to cochair the department until one or both of them left.

Like Dr. Everly had done, Jessica printed off a copy of the ultrasound. "As far as due dates go, I really don't want to put a specific time to it, since we probably won't be able to let you go to full term. It's a balancing act of giving those babies all the time we can to develop and gain weight, while not compromising your health or theirs. Does that make sense?"

"It does. I'm assuming I'll have to have a cesarean?"

"It's what I prefer for higher-order multiples. Especially given your age and the fertility issues you've had in the past." She leaned over and nudged Bella's shoulder with her own. "And believe me, when I say the word *age* I don't mean anything bad by it. You're still young and vibrant. As long as you try to stay in shape and not gain weight too rapidly, we should be good to go."

"I'll do my best. We were already talking about going to the Bosques de Palermo on a regular basis to get some exercise." She glanced up at Seb and he nodded back. "I really want these babies. I won't do anything to jeopardize the pregnancy."

Okay, just when he'd started thinking she wasn't planning on shutting him out entirely, since she was including him when she talked about going to the park, she switched gears and went back to speaking in terms of herself.

That was another thing they probably needed to hash out. Was he allowed to give input when he felt she was working too hard? When he felt she was doing something that put her or the babies at risk? Like with their overdose patient?

Jessica looked from one to the other. "Let's go at this like a team, shall we? You and Sebastián work together, and if either of you have any questions about whether something is safe or not, you come to me and ask." She smiled. "And don't worry. Sex is definitely not off the table. At least not for now. But when we get down to the end, we'll have to start putting limits on some things like nipple stimulation and so forth."

What the hell? Nipple stimulation?

The specialist was nothing if not forthright. But then again, the woman had no idea that for all intents and purposes he and Bella were separated and that sex was not only *not* on the table, but not on any other piece of furniture either.

He didn't even want it to be unless it meant something. Not like during their later attempts at pregnancy, when it had lost some of that meaning. Seb had never been one to just sleep with someone in order to gain a physical release. He wanted an emotional connection with his partner. And right now, he and Bella didn't have that.

He let go of her hand on the pretext of doing something with his sock. He couldn't blame Dr. Lucas for assuming they were a loving couple. Sitting here together, holding hands, they were certainly the picture of one. But unless Bella disabused her of the notion, he wasn't going to say anything. He was pretty sure the specialist would look askance at that. It might even add some points to whatever mental risk chart she used to assess patients. Seb didn't want to do anything that would hurt Bella's chances at having three healthy babies. He'd move out of the apartment before he let that happen.

"Do you have any other questions? About intimacy or anything else?"

"No. None."

Bella's quick answer made it pretty clear that she didn't want to go into any details about that aspect of their life. Not that they really had one anymore.

"Fair enough. If you do have something you want to know, feel free to call the office and leave me a message. I always try to get back to my patients by the end of the day." She handed Seb the printed image of their babies and wiped the transponder down with alcohol before tucking it back in its holder, switching off the machine. Then she stood up. "Well, it's been nice finally getting to meet you both. I want to see you pretty soon. Honestly, I'd like to try to get a look at that third fetus, just to make sure everything is okay with him or her. So in another week or two? Does that work for you?"

Seb looked at Bella. "It does for me, how about you?" He added, "As far as your work schedule goes, that is." To make it clear that that was all that mattered.

She nodded. "We'll figure it out. I'd also like to know if they're boys or girls, if it's okay with you."

"It is." He glanced at the doctor. "We'll work on names, although I can't make any promises that we'll come to any hard and fast decisions by then."

"No hard and fast decisions needed. There is no need to stress about things like that. Just have fun with it. And each other." She gave a meaningful wink then said, "I'll see you soon."

Just have fun with it and each other.

Her meaning couldn't have been any more plain. He gave an internal eye roll. Little did the woman know that this whole process had been stressful. And if it was for him, then it had to be doubly hard for Bella, who was actually carrying their babies.

It was up to him to make sure he didn't add to that stress. No matter how hard that might prove to be. Maybe it was time to do something about that.

"Do you have time for some coffee or some lunch?"

Bella smiled. "I don't drink coffee anymore, remember? But I am starving, actually. Can we stop somewhere for a quick bite?"

"Yep. I know just the place."

The place turned out to be one of their old haunts. An Italian eatery that boasted wonderful food and quick service. They used to come here all the time in happier days. They went through the doors and one of the waiters hurried by only to retrace his steps. "Signor and Signora Lopez. Welcome back. It has been too long."

Bella smiled. "Yes, it has, Matteo." It had been more than a year since they'd eaten here. It was funny how little by little things had changed, going almost unnoticed at first, until it was impossible to ignore that their relationship was in trouble. It still was. But it was nice to visit a little bit of the past. A place where she'd felt safe and loved. She was suddenly glad Seb had brought her here.

Without realizing it, her hand went under her belly as if reassuring herself that the babies were still there—just as safe and loved. Then she realized the waiter was staring at her, obviously wanting to ask, but probably wondering if it would appear rude to.

"Yes. We're expecting."

He clapped Seb on the back. "*Congratulazioni!* Come with me. I will get you a table in a nice little corner. Very *romantica*."

"Oh, but..." But the waiter was already walking away, glancing back to make sure they were following him. She looked at Seb to see laughter in his eyes. She swatted at his arm. "Not funny."

She followed the waiter, and sure enough they were seated in a quiet corner. But maybe that was better. Nothing they said could be overheard. Especially if things turned heated or seemed out of place for a couple who were expecting a child and were supposed to be in love. She suddenly wanted a drink.

"Ugh, I wish I could at least have a glass of wine. They have a Chianti that I love."

"I seem to remember a time when two glasses would make you slightly tipsy."

She laughed. "I remember that too. Except I seem to remember that I wasn't always *too* tipsy."

There was a marked pause. "No. You weren't." The words were soft, and she realized he remembered those times as well. It was before they'd started trying to have kids. They'd go home and make love, except she always fell asleep right afterwards. Seb used to tell her he loved her little snuffling snores that happened when she'd had a little too much to drink.

Matteo came to take their drink and lunch order, already seeming to know that she would need something sparkling rather than alcoholic, while Seb chose to have a house ale. "I'll be back with your drinks and have your food out quickly."

They thanked him.

"I'd forgotten how nice this place was."

"Me, too." There was a short pause. "So, names. Do you have any ideas, yet?"

"No. I haven't really given it much thought. Until now. But I guess we should start looking. How about you?"

He shook his head. "No. Not at all."

"Okay, so that's something we should get together and talk about. I think I have a book somewhere."

She knew right where that book was but didn't want it to bring back any bad memories. Not when things seemed to be going better than they had in a while. So she quickly changed the subject. "What was the name of the other waiter that took our order quite often?"

"Mmm…" He seemed to think for a minute. "I think it starts with a *P*?"

"Paolo?"

"Yes, that was it. He used to flirt with you."

"He did not." She stared at him.

Seb leaned forward, his dark eyes on hers. "Yes. He most definitely did. But I can't blame him."

"I don't remember that at all. I just remember him being nice."

"Matteo is nice. Paolo…well, he was nice in a different way." He grinned. "I'm glad you didn't notice."

A small shiver went through her. "Why is that?"

His fingers touched hers for a second. "Because then I might have had to put a stop to it."

"As if I couldn't do it myself?" She tried to sound indignant, but there was something funny swirling around in her stomach. A weird yearning or something that was like… happiness. An emotion that used to come so easily for them.

"You could definitely do it yourself. But you didn't know what he was doing. So…" He lifted a shoulder in a shrug. "While he flirted, I had the pleasure of knowing that I was the one you'd be going home with."

She swallowed. She had no idea Seb had thoughts like that. But there was something sexy about it. About the pride in his voice when he said that.

"I never wanted to go home with anyone else." She couldn't have stopped the words if she'd tried. Because they were true.

"I'm glad." His fingers came up to cup her cheek, and a shivery longing came over her. His glance fell to her lips, and the world seemed to tilt on its axis.

He was going to kiss her.

His hand moved to her nape, and he slowly drew her forward, her lips parting even as he leaned closer. The lines of his cheeks stood out in sharp relief in the dim light of the lamp on the wall, and she reveled in the fact that this beautiful man had once loved her deeply. Surely she could enjoy this one little moment.

Her eyelids fluttered closed as his warm breath grazed her mouth.

Suddenly a loud crashing sound reverberated through the space, followed by cursing in two different languages. Angry voices grew in volume.

They sprang apart, and Bella saw that across the restaurant a waiter had dropped a whole tray of food, causing a huge uproar.

The mood was lost, and they sat there looking at each other awkwardly for a long moment before they sat back in their seats.

Matteo appeared with their drinks a second later.

Well, Seb wasn't indifferent to her, that was for sure.

It was what she'd wanted, wasn't it?

Except that in the sheltered light of an Italian restaurant, things could appear very soft and diaphanous. Very *romantica*, as Matteo had put it. But in the harsh reality of the world outside of this space?

Things didn't always last. If Bella didn't want her heart broken all over again, she needed to be careful. Very very careful. Because she'd witnessed firsthand how things could change, going from wonderful to unbearably sad in a matter of months. And she wasn't sure she could risk going back to visit the sexy, loving moments, knowing they could quickly morph into something they might both come to regret.

CHAPTER FIVE

THE SLIGHT CREAK of the door behind her made her stiffen with the pen and notebook still in hand. It was still fairly early in the morning, and she'd come out onto their balcony while the air was still and cool. She realized today that she didn't come out here nearly as much as she should. Or as much as she used to. There was something particularly quiet and peaceful about the city in the morning. A week had passed since their time at the restaurant, and she was still shaken by how close she'd been to giving in to her feelings.

Sitting on a rattan settee with her feet tucked under her, she'd been perusing a book of baby names and jotting down the ones that struck her as possibilities.

Bella glanced to the side and saw Seb standing in the open doorway, his tall frame taking up most of the space.

"Everything okay?" he asked.

She nodded. "Just following doctors' orders." She held the book up so that he could see the title.

"Baby names. I guess you are. I didn't even realize you had that."

She licked her lips, not sure how to tell him that she'd bought the book six or seven cycles ago, when her hopes for a successful treatment had still been fresh. "I've had it for a while."

He didn't say anything to that; instead, he just moved further out onto the balcony and sat on a chair across from her. "Do you have any ideas about what you want to call them?"

"Yes, and I'd like to get your opinion. Can you scoot your chair around here?"

He pulled his chair next to the settee while she moved so that she was sitting fairly close to him. It would have been easier for him to just join her on it, and in the old days he wouldn't have hesitated, but since the restaurant it was like they both wanted a separation between them that was both physical and emotional.

Putting the notebook on her lap, she turned it so that he could see it. She'd put two columns on it, one for boys and one for girls. She'd starred the ones that were her current favorites. "Do you want to look at the book itself?"

He gave a crooked smile that made her chest hurt. "It looks like you have almost a whole book's worth of names already written down."

The way he smiled had always made her slightly woozy, and she'd once considered herself the luckiest woman in the world to be married to someone like him. Suddenly aware of her ratty old nightshirt and the hair she hadn't brushed, she put a hand up to run her fingers through the tangled locks. "That might be a slight exaggeration."

He made a sound. "Very slight."

She couldn't hold back her laugh. This *was* like old times. Times when she hadn't felt self-conscious about the way she looked in the mornings. Times when they'd been in sync about everything down to the stuff that other people would find unimportant. But to her it had always just showed how compatible they were.

And their lovemaking. *Dios*. Even without the wine, it had always sent her into the stratosphere no matter how long they'd been married. Sometimes gentle, sometimes frantic, no two times were alike. At least that's the way it had been up until the last couple of years, when things had become robotic and awkward. Just going through the motions to get to where they wanted her to be: pregnant.

Now here she was. They'd reached their goal. But for what? The success wasn't quite as sweet as she'd imagined it to be. Maybe that's because she'd never imagined their relationship getting to the place it was now. And it made her incredibly sad.

He reached over and pointed to one of the names on the list. "Luis. That's my dad's name."

"I know. I chose it because of that."

Seb leaned back and seemed to stare through the wrought iron railing of the balcony not saying anything for a minute or two, but she knew he was touched. Last year Seb's dad had been diagnosed with leukemia. It was in remission currently, but there was no telling how long that would last or if it would come back with a vengeance. It reminded her that she doubted if his parents knew about the pregnancy, although she'd already told her mom and stepdad. Her mom hadn't been super happy about Seb's absence, and Bella had found herself coming to his defense saying he'd already had the trip planned—even though that was one of the things that had hurt her the most.

"Have you told your mom and dad yet?"

He looked at her. "No. I wasn't sure how to explain why we waited so long to let them know."

It hadn't been Seb who'd waited so long, it had been her. Her fear of telling Seb after he'd seemed so adamant about not trying again. Her fear that he'd already decided their marriage was over and that to tell him now would just cement that decision or worse, that he'd stay with her only because of the babies—something that seemingly had come true. The way he'd almost recoiled when the doctor had mentioned sex had taken her aback, although she'd had much the same reaction to Dr. Lucas's blunt words.

Even hearing the comment about stimulation had made her nipples react. She evidently didn't need him to touch her for that to happen.

"Do you want to invite them over to dinner to tell them?"

He shook his head. "I don't want you having to fix a meal, and we both know that my culinary skills are pretty rudimentary."

"Your mom loves to cook. I'm sure the mere mention of getting together for dinner will send her into planning mode."

The fact that Helena loved entertaining had always taken a huge load off her, and Bella loved them both dearly. The thought of them not being in her life anymore made her sad. Even though they would always be the triplets' grandparents, once she and Seb were divorced things would inevitably change between them. She'd no longer be invited to family meals or to go on family trips together.

Why was she so certain they would divorce?

Because the thought of him staying in a loveless marriage just for the sake of the children was unbearable. He deserved to fall in love again and find happiness, even if it wasn't with her—something that seemed just as unbearable as him staying married to her.

There was no winning, it seemed.

"Do you want me to call her?"

"Would you? My parents already know." Bella's biological dad had passed away five years ago in a traffic accident, just at the start of their fertility journey. But it was just as well. It would be hard to see him and think that her life was going down the same path that his once had.

Seb didn't say anything about her parents already knowing, but his mouth tightened.

She couldn't blame him. He'd had a right to be the first one to hear the news and instead, she'd told her mom and dad while keeping the babies' own father in dark.

She reached out and touched his hand. "I'm sorry, Seb. Truly. Looking back, I realize I should have returned your call. I was scared about how you would react since you were so certain that we shouldn't try again."

"When I came home and you finally did tell me, I thought you'd kept it a secret because you'd found someone else. You have no idea how that made me feel."

The fact that he was bringing this up again spoke to how deeply that had affected him. But her pain over the fact that he'd thought she'd been unfaithful was just as sharp. They'd hurt each other without even trying. It made her wary of sharing things with him, of thinking too much about the what-ifs or the realities of their situation.

"You're right, I don't. At the time it felt like the right thing to do, but I can see now that it wasn't. All I can do is say how sorry I am."

"It's over and done now." He squeezed her hand and let it go. "So what other names do we have here?"

She glanced down at the paper again and

pointed. "My dad's name is here too, of course." Her stepdad's, that was. He'd been there every step of the way for her; his love for a child who wasn't his flesh and blood was strong and undeniable.

"So, Sergio and Luis. Those should definitely stay. And if we have two girls and one boy?"

"We could still use both names. One for the first name and one for the middle name."

That made him smile again, and she did her best not to stare. Again. But it was hard. She'd always loved looking at his face. She knew it so well that she dreamed about him in living color. And some of those dreams were X-rated. It sometimes made it hard to face him in the morning, because the stuff he'd done to her in her sleep made her blush. She knew most of that was hormones; she'd read in one of her pregnancy books that the second trimester brought renewed interest in sex, and it hadn't been kidding. She wanted it. Wanted him, despite the fact that they were still not in a good place.

But maybe they could be… After all, being at the restaurant with him last week had made her take another look at things like that.

Seriously? If he was only here for the babies, how could they have a normal relationship knowing that he had very little interest in her as a person, just about what was growing inside of her? Sex wasn't always about love, wasn't that what people said?

She glanced at him, but his eyes were on the list she'd made. "I like Lorenzo and Gilberto as well," he said.

"Lorenzo is also one of my favorites."

"Okay, I'm good with Luis, Sergio and Lorenzo for boys' names, then. How about you?"

"Yes. That works." She liked the idea of having two names that represented their fathers.

She pointed at two names from the girls' side as well. "I have Helena and Rute after our moms. We could do the same if we only have one girl and call her Helena Rute Lopez."

Bella was proud of herself. She hadn't even hesitated at saying Lopez and knew if they did divorce, she wouldn't go back to her maiden name. No matter what the future held, she'd loved her life with him and wasn't anxious to remove all traces of their past, although she completely understood why many women did.

She still loved Seb. She probably always would. What she didn't love was the thought of living the rest of her life with him, if he no longer felt the same way about her. And she doubted he did. That last scene before he'd left for Angola had caused a breach in their relationship that she wasn't sure could ever be healed. She had learned a lesson from it, though. She would never plead with him for anything again. After he'd left, she'd sat there feeling humiliated and broken. A lot of that had to do with her and not Seb. And a month after he'd left, her sadness had turned to an anger so palpable that she'd been surprised it hadn't hurt her pregnancy. Shock, sadness, disbelief, bargaining, anger, resignation. Weren't those all stages of grief? She'd hit every one of those milestones during his absence, and now she was in a no-man's-land of resignation.

"What other girls' names are your favorites?"

His question made her shake off her melancholic thoughts. She was pregnant with babies she thought she'd never have. She needed to be grateful rather than wallowing in self-pity.

Yes, from now on she was going to think about her children and not about what might have been with Seb. Wouldn't it have been worse to lose the babies *and* him?

Yes, it would. So she looked down at the

list and rattled off a few names and listened to him counter them, adding Sara to the mix when he said it was one of his favorites.

After about a half hour of lighthearted negotiating and some laughter that she took joy in, they had their short list of names. "So I guess we wait until the next appointment with Jessica when hopefully she will be able to tell us the gender of all of them. Including the shy one."

"The shy one. It'll be interesting to see if that carries over after he's born. Hopefully he or she will feel like coming out to play, at least for the ultrasound. Then we can present the list to my parents."

"Let me know when they want to get together. I work days this week and nights next, so if we can schedule it in in the next few days, maybe at the very end of the week, that would probably be ideal."

"Okay, I'll work on it." He slid his palm behind her neck, easing her close enough to give her a quick kiss on the forehead.

A thousand emotions went through her at his touch, the worst of which was hope. It was just muscle memory. Things he'd done hundreds of times in the past—a habit built over ten years of marriage. It had to be. But it made her want to cry.

When he pulled away, he looked just as shell-shocked as she felt. He stood with a quick "see you sometime tonight" and left the room without another word.

She sat there for a long time, the list and book forgotten as she tried to relegate things like kisses on the forehead to the past. Because it was unlikely that it would happen again. It was also unlikely that she'd invite it to happen again, since it would just bring up painful feelings. Like longing and hope for the future. She needed to reserve those emotions for her babies. Because to do anything else would only be inviting disaster. And it could very well send her into a pit of despair all over again.

Seb had gone out on that balcony not realizing that Bella was even out there. But once he'd opened the door, it had been too late to withdraw without coming up with a plausible explanation. One he didn't have on hand.

When she'd looked up at him, her cheeks had been flushed with healthy color and the light that poured into the space had made her hair gleam in a way that seemed almost otherworldly. Pregnancy agreed with her. The book and her list had been in her lap, and her hand and arm had been draped protectively over the slight curve of her belly. It could have competed with a painting in any museum and probably would have come out the winner.

She was beautiful and…happy. And none of that had anything to do with him. In fact, she'd seemed to dim when he entered her orbit. The babies were enough for her, and he needed to accept that fact, as hard as it was.

Hell, if she lost them now she'd be devastated. So would he, but she seemed to be pinning all of her hopes and dreams on these tiny creatures and he couldn't blame her. She'd wanted motherhood for as long as he could remember.

All he could do was help make sure that her dreams came true, and that meant protecting her as much as possible…easing the way as much as he could.

He'd caught sight of her at work when he arrived at the hospital an hour early for his shift, and unlike normal days when Bella seemed to thrive on the unpredictable nature of the ER, she seemed tired. More tired than normal. It was enough that he walked over to her to ask if she was okay.

Before he could open his mouth, though, someone tapped him on the back, and when he turned, he saw one of the other ER residents standing there looking at them with a beaming smile. "I just heard. I'm so happy for you both. Congratulations!"

Bella raised her head and gave the man a tired smile. "Thank you. We appreciate it."

"Yes," Seb agreed. "We do."

With that, he stepped in between the other doctor and Bella, hoping the man got the hint and went on his way, although the move probably came across as rude. It worked, though. The doctor threw them another smile and continued down the hallway.

"Has that been happening all day?"

"Yep. I let it be known to a couple of friends that I was pregnant, since we agreed not to keep it a secret any longer. Well, the news seems to have spread like wildfire, although it was going to be obvious pretty soon. My clothes are getting tighter by the day."

"I'm sorry. I don't know how to make it better."

Her brows went up. "The clothes part? I don't think there's much hope of that."

His gaze swept over her, and his lips twitched.

"No, I meant all the congratulations that will probably come our way."

"Me either. They're going to assume it means we're back together." She gave a tired laugh. "I don't think we ever told people we were separated in the first place, although it was probably pretty obvious that something was wrong by the end."

He really didn't want to get into a discussion about the state of their relationship here in the hallway of the hospital. Actually, he didn't want to get into that discussion anywhere. Not when he hadn't quite figured things out himself yet. Part of him was dreading the babies' births because it meant that they would probably go their separate ways, dividing one household into two.

Stop going down that road.

Instead, he said, "Why don't I go ahead and start my shift now. You look run off your feet. You can go home and relax."

"That bad, huh?" She smiled, though, and this time it seemed genuine. "It doesn't matter. I'm actually going to take you up on your offer if you're serious. I am pretty tired. It's been hectic today and with all of the well-wishers…"

"Let me fend them off for a while. I'm sure

in a day or two, everyone will get it out of their system, and it will become old news."

At least until they broke up for real.

"Thanks. Do you mind if I head to the office and unwind a little?"

Even though the office had both of their names on the door and they were both head of the department, Seb normally did the day-to-day paperwork for the ER and used the space a lot more than she did. "Of course not. Why don't you stretch out on the couch for a bit?"

He wasn't even going to picture that, because it would lead to other thoughts that were best left for another time. Actually they were best relegated to the past, where they belonged.

The urge to kiss her on the forehead, like he had on the balcony, came and went. He'd made that mistake this morning, and it had not been a smart move. The taste of her skin was something he would never get out of his system. And kissing her had just reminded him of too many things that would likely never happen again. Like sleeping tangled so tightly together that he was never sure where he ended and she began. Worse was how uncomfortable she'd looked when he'd pulled away this morning. It had been a mistake, and it seemed they both knew exactly how much of one. So no more kissing.

He only hoped he could remember how *not* to do that. How *not* to do a lot of things. So he just said, "Go get some rest. I'll check on you in a little while."

"If your shift is anything like mine, you won't have time to. Don't worry, I'll set my alarm. Unlike you, I don't keep a second set of clothes here at the hospital."

Many doctors did, but Bella only kept a second set of scrubs in case of contamination. She'd always insisted she was going home to change and that she wasn't going to spend the nights at the hospital like Seb had on numerous occasions. It was one of the few things they'd really disagreed on and looking back at it, he saw just how many moments he'd missed with her by not coming home. How many opportunities to hold her had come and gone. Now he would never get them back again.

He rubbed at a phantom pain in his chest that just wouldn't leave. "Just for the record, you're right not to."

"I am?" She blinked a couple of times as if unsure why he was suddenly saying that. But he wasn't going to admit to her that she'd been right all along. About more than just that.

The realization that it was too little, too late and would change nothing did not ease that gnawing ache.

He caught sight of another staff member hurrying toward them and he said, "Go. Save yourself. While you still can."

She glanced in the direction he was looking and laughed. "You don't have to tell me twice." With that, she spun around and headed in the direction of their office while he did his best to smile and accept the person's happy thoughts on his and Bella's news. Only this person spelled out that he was simply happy to see them together.

It went on like that for the rest of the evening—varying messages with the same theme. And when he'd taken his break at midnight and went to check on Bella, the office was empty. She must have gone home like she said she would. He was glad. She'd sleep better in her own bed.

In *their* own bed. Heaven knew he wasn't getting much rest in the guest room, and it had nothing to do with the comfort of the mattress. It had to do with knowing she was just out of reach in the bedroom down the hall.

Sighing, he noted the indent of her body was still on the couch, and a knitted throw—a gift from his mom—was lying loosely folded on the cushion rather than draped over the back of it like it normally was. Unable to resist, he lay down where she'd been and closed his eyes. He should at least call Bella to let her know where he was, but then again, he'd often ended up sleeping in his office, and he didn't want to wake her if she was already at home asleep.

Sucking down a deep breath, he allowed himself to settle more deeply into the quiet of the night. Into the quiet of not having to run from emergency to emergency with barely time to breathe. And after a few minutes, he let his muscles relax one by one, his last thought being that he needed to call his mom in the morning.

His mom answered on the second ring. "Hi, Seb. This is early for you, isn't it?"

"A little." No need to tell the truth that he'd spent most of last night being hounded by person after person all ecstatic that he and Bella were not only pregnant, but evidently back together. He couldn't blame them, and he probably would have done the same if he'd been in their position. A few more months of this, though, and things were going to be a mess to straighten out. "But I have a question for you. Do you and Dad have time for us to come over for a visit?"

"Of course, you don't even have to ask. Can we do a meal? Bella looked a little wan the last time I saw her at the hospital."

"You came to see her?"

"We did, about a month ago. You were in Africa, and I wanted to make sure she had everything she needed. She was busy and didn't have a lot of time for chitchat. We agreed to meet for coffee, but we could never work out a good time."

Maybe because Bella didn't want to explain why she wasn't drinking coffee at the moment, even though she loved it. Her mom knew that she'd abstained from it while trying to get pregnant, but with Seb in Africa there would have been no reason for her not to drink it. He couldn't blame her for wanting to avoid that conversation, especially knowing that she hadn't even told Seb that he was going to be a father.

"Well, we have the time now. Would sometime at the end of this week work?"

"Absolutely. How about Friday?"

They had an appointment that morning with the specialist, but they were free that evening, since both of them were off. "Perfect. Want us to bring anything?"

"How about a bottle of wine?" There was a pause before her mom added, "If you guys are trying to get pregnant again, I'll understand if you'd rather not do that."

But this was one explanation he didn't want to attempt. Not without Bella at his side. "Nope, we're not currently trying. So wine it is." It wasn't a complete lie.

"Is there anything special you want?"

He'd never thought to ask Bella if there was anything in particular that she was avoiding. He knew there were certain foods she shouldn't eat during her pregnancy, so to be safe, he simply said, "Make your roast chicken dish. You know it's always been one of Bella's favorite things."

As well as nipple stimulation…

Damn! Why had that thought come to mind?

"Great. I'm happy you guys can come. Do you realize I haven't even seen you since you got back?"

He did realize it. But it was also something he'd been kind of avoiding, not wanting to go into any deep discussions on the state of his marriage. His mom had always been especially intuitive about those kinds of things. She would have probably read him like a book. So yes. Better to face his parents together. “Dad still doing okay?”

“He is. His last checkup still showed no signs of any abnormal cells in his blood.”

Seb gave a sigh of relief and counted his blessings. He might wish some things in his life were different, but not this. He was hopeful his dad would have many, many more years of health.

“Give him a hug for me, and we’ll see you guys on Friday.”

“See you then, Sebito.”

The diminutive of his name made him smile as it always did. He was head and shoulders taller than his mom, but she still called him “Little Seb.” Yes, he was blessed in so many ways. So maybe he should start focusing on that and not on all the ways he wished things were different. Because they weren’t. And hoping for the impossible would do no one any good.

One thing he and Bella did need to talk about was how to approach Friday’s dinner. They’d always been a fairly demonstrative couple, and his mom would notice if there were no longer any little touches to the hand and arm, no upturned lips waiting for him to drop a kiss on them. And if his mom noticed, there was no way she would let it go by without saying something or asking him what was wrong.

So did they tell her the truth, that he was only living with Bella to help her with the pregnancy and delivery? Or did they put on the performance of a lifetime and hope that somehow his mom bought it? At least until after the babies were born and they could figure out exactly how to break his mother's heart.

CHAPTER SIX

THEIR SHIFTS JUST so happened to align a few days later. He'd had to go to a meeting at another hospital for a day and in the scramble to cover everything, he hadn't thought about the fact that Bella would be working at the same time he was.

Trying to stagger their shifts probably wasn't one of his smartest moves, because they still saw each other at home.

But at almost eighteen and a half weeks pregnant now, the changes in her were becoming more and more obvious. And not just her growing abdomen.

It wasn't anything she did or said so much as a paleness that seemed to hover over her whenever there was a case that required her to exert herself. He made a mental note to ask the specialist about it and see if Bella maybe needed to start cutting back on her hours. She wasn't carrying just one baby—she was carrying three. Surely that was three times the strain on her system?

They still hadn't discussed this upcoming Friday night and how she wanted to play it. But he would have to broach that subject soon as well.

Thankfully it looked like most of the people he knew or were acquainted with had gotten the congratulations thing out of their system.

"Dr. Lopez to the ER. Dr. Sebastián Lopez, please come to the emergency department."

His heart stopped for a second. Bella? Had something happened? He'd just sat down to do some paperwork when the call came in, and he jumped out of his seat and sprinted down the hallway to find Bella crouched on top of a moving gurney administering CPR to a patient. What the hell? What did she think she was doing?

He caught up with the group and said, "Switch with me."

Bella glanced up with a frown and motioned him away, not losing a beat. He followed them, noting she was practically panting with the next set of chest compressions. He didn't want to overstep, but it was obvious she couldn't keep this up for much longer. He was just about to insist when she looked at him.

"Okay," she said, "Switch."

She scrambled down from the gurney, and Seb leaned in and took over compressions with Bella squeezing the Ambu bag, still slightly out of breath as she rattled off the symptoms. "Thirty-two-year-old man suffering electrocution while trying to illegally hook into the city's power grid. Immediate cardiac arrest and serious electric burns to both hands."

The burns were the least of the man's worries. At this point they'd be lucky to even get his heart started again. "Defibrillated?" He had to say the word between compressions.

"Twice en route. They got a rhythm twice as well, but he arrested again within a minute each time."

The fact that they'd even gotten something gave Seb enough hope to continue lifesaving measures. If his heart had sustained irreparable damage, it was doubtful they'd get him back at all.

They got him into one of the rooms and evidently the trauma department had already been assembled because Sofia Martinez—one of the group's surgeons—was waiting there with her team. One of those doctors stepped up to take over compressions.

Sofia glanced at them. "A cardiac specialist is on his way down. How long has he been in arrest?"

"Twenty-five minutes." Bella repeated what she'd been told as she hooked up the leads for the heart monitor. "They got him back twice for short stretches only to have him relapse. Let's get a central line in and administer one milligram epinephrine."

It's what he would have suggested as well, and he noted Sofia was also nodding.

A nurse got the line in and another prepared and injected the requested dosage, even as external CPR continued. Everyone's eyes were on the monitor next to the bed.

What was barely a squiggle suddenly came alive with blips and sharp peaks within a minute of the epi being delivered. "Cease CPR," said Sophia.

The person administering compressions stopped, and the rhythm persisted. Everyone held their breath waiting to see if it would stop again. But it didn't. And while the tracing didn't look exactly normal, it didn't look nearly as hopeless as it had a minute or two earlier.

Just then, Dr. Gilead pushed into the room,

eyes immediately going to the monitor. "You got him back."

"Yes," Sofia said. "For now."

The cardiac specialist's lips were tight as he perused the scene. "Let's try to keep that momentum going. The patient was electrocuted, is that correct?"

Bella spoke up. "Yes. Catastrophic burns to his hands, but he was blown off the transformer pretty quickly, so it looks like exposure was limited although it was from a higher voltage."

Dr. Gilead glanced at the man's limbs and gave a soft whistle. "I want to get an echo to look for damage to the heart. It might be beating at the moment, but if it's sustained the same amount of damage as those hands… Well, I'd rather know it now than put hours into him if there's no chance whatsoever for survival."

"Agreed," said Sofia.

Although it sounded heartless on the surface, Dr. Gilead and Sofia knew what they were talking about. The didn't want a patient to suffer needlessly if there was no hope. None of them did.

Now that the case had been handed off

from the ER team to the trauma and cardiology units, there was really no reason for Seb or Bella to stick around. But Seb was curious about the case and wanted to know the outcome. From the way Bella was hanging at the back of the room, she felt the same way.

Dr. Gilead again looked at the man's hands as the echocardiogram equipment was being set up and shook his head. "Let's just hope that what's on the inside doesn't look as bad as the outside."

No one was even talking about the mangled condition of the man's hands. If he made it, it was doubtful they could save them. The current had ripped through one hand and out the other with the exit burn looking even more horrific than the entry wound. Seb couldn't even tell where his fingers were supposed to be on that one.

Fifteen minutes later, they had their answer. The heart looked intact and his values were now almost within normal limits, although Dr. Gilead said there were a few troubling PVCs happening every few minutes. They would need to wait and see if they progressed to another series of arrhythmias or if they righted themselves.

"Let's get him up to ICU. Does anyone know if his family has been notified?"

Bella again spoke up. "His wife is out in the waiting room. She's the one who called for the EMTs after the accident. She started CPR."

"He was lucky she knew how, or he probably wouldn't be here right now. Can either you or Seb go out and update her while we work to get him stable? Once that happens I'll give her another update."

Bella nodded. "Not a problem."

Seb frowned. She was looking more and more exhausted by the minute. Friday morning they had their next appointment with Jessica so she could try to get a look at baby number three and to see if she could determine the gender of all three babies, and while he wouldn't override Bella, he would like to ask the specialist how much she could expect her body to do. And for how long.

Because right now she looked like she was at her limit, much as she had the other day when he'd offered to finish her shift. Surely she could see that it wasn't healthy for her or the babies to continue to push herself like this?

Once they got in the hallway, he said, "I can go talk with his wife."

She glanced at him with a frown. "I'm quite capable of talking with family members."

Did she think he was questioning her ability to do her job? That hadn't been his intention, but then again a lot of what he did nowadays seemed to be wrong, and he wasn't sure how to correct course, or if he should even try.

"I know you can. I just meant that you look exhausted."

"So do you. But that doesn't mean you shouldn't still be here working."

He touched her arm. "Hey, stop for a minute, please."

She did as he asked and turned to look at him. "What?"

"I'm not criticizing you. I'm just worried, Bella. Worried you won't know when to stop. Worried you'll push yourself too hard."

Her eyes shut for a long minute, and she lifted her hands and used her fingertips to rub slow circles on her temple area. She had a headache. She got them periodically, and he used to be the one who did this for her.

Without asking, he went behind her and pushed her hands out of the way and used his own fingers to apply slow, steady pressure to the sides of her face, moving from her temples to her cheeks and back up again.

"Mmm...feels good."

Someone went by them and smiled at them. Seb ignored them. It didn't matter what people thought or didn't think. What did matter was that Bella was in obvious distress.

She let him continue for a few more minutes before drawing in a deep breath and then blowing it out. "Thank you. We'd better go, though."

Coming back to stand in front of her, he used his fingertips to tip her chin up. "When we're done with the family, I want you to do something for me, okay?"

Her eyes flew open and met his. He couldn't stop his own smile. "It's nothing like that. I just want to take your blood pressure and make sure it's normal."

She bit her lip. "I didn't even think about that. I have had a low-grade headache most of the day, but just assumed I slept wrong."

The fact that she wasn't putting up a fight or telling him he was being ridiculous concerned him even more. There was a bigger risk of preeclampsia in women carrying multiples, although it was still a little early in the pregnancy.

"So you'll let me?"

"Yes. I think it's just tiredness, but if it'll make you feel better, I'll go along with it."

"Just humor me, okay? I'm sure it's nothing, but I'd rather not take a chance, and I know Jessica would agree with me."

"I know she would, too."

A few minutes after they'd spoken with their patient's wife and grown son, they found themselves in an exam room. Seb wrapped the cuff around Bella's upper arm and pumped the pressure up until he could get a reading. Letting the air slowly hiss out, he watched the numbers until they reached the bottom. "One-thirty over eighty. Not terrible, but a little higher than yours normally runs."

"And you would know that how?"

His brows lifted. "I know."

Her eyes left his and stared at the wall. "The ER has been short-staffed the last couple of days and…" She shrugged.

"Why didn't you say anything?" In the same way that he did much of the ER's paperwork, Bella was more people-oriented and kept her finger on the pulse of the department's workforce. "You cannot take everything on yourself. Especially not right now."

"I know. It's just who I am. It's hard to turn it off and walk away."

Her words couldn't have described their situation any better. It was hard to just turn off his feelings and walk away from what they'd once meant to each other. "I get it. More than you know."

When her glance came up and met his, she sighed and shook her head. "What happened to us, Seb?"

He brushed her hair back from the sides of her face, his fingers cupping her cheeks. "I don't know, Bell. I wish to hell I did."

They stayed like that for what seemed like an eternity, with her sitting on the exam table and him standing next to her. The blood pressure cuff was still around her arm, but that wasn't what caught his attention. It was the way she was looking at him. Like she was feeling sad and hopeless—like she'd lost her way in this world. Maybe because since they'd met they'd always made this journey through life together. And now neither one of them knew quite which way to turn.

His thumbs stroked along the sides of her face, and she closed her eyes, the sounds of her breathing soft in the room. She was just so damned gorgeous.

Before he could stop himself, he leaned down to give her a soft kiss on the lips, more as a way to reassure her than anything. At least that's what he told himself.

But when she sighed again and didn't pull away, he allowed himself to stay, the pressure of his mouth increasing slightly, his fingers sliding into the hair at her nape. He massaged her scalp, even as he let his lips slide away and then come back for another taste.

Then when her hands slid up to his shoulders he pressed closer, turning her to face him, reveling in the feel of her mouth opening to his.

It was like he'd never kissed this woman before in his life. He was aware of everything about her. The way she smelled of soap and clean air, despite the fact that she'd been working around hospital antiseptic most of the day. The way her mouth clung so sweetly to his in a way that he had trouble remembering it ever doing before.

He kissed along her cheek and moved to her ear, "Bella, *Dios*, I—"

Just then the sound of the door opening, made him jerk back so fast that he heard the Velcro on the pressure cuff rip apart. He turned toward the door to see one of the nurses retreating with an apologetic smile on her face.

Damn. He had no doubt that news would soon be all over the hospital that she'd seen the husband-and-wife team making out in an exam room.

When his glance returned to Bella, he saw that she'd hopped down the from the table. "What were we thinking?"

He didn't know what she was thinking, but he knew exactly what he'd been thinking. That he'd been caught up in the moment and in the memories of what they'd once been. Of what they'd once meant to each other. Except that was a fantasy. A fantasy that hadn't had its roots in reality for a very long time.

"I'm sorry, Bella. I was worried and wanted to reassure you. Obviously, I forgot myself."

Instead of saying she'd been caught up in the moment as well, she pulled the pressure cuff the rest of the way off with a sharp sound and tossed it onto the table. "It can't happen again, Seb. It just…can't. I can't go through this again. It hurts too much. Okay?"

He nodded, a lump in his throat growing until it was hard to breathe. Only then did he realize the depths of the pain he'd put her through. How she must have felt abandoned by him not only physically, but emotionally. And in reality he had done both. In trying to protect himself—and her, he'd told himself—he'd allowed his actions to devastate the woman he'd once loved with all of his heart. The woman he'd sworn never to hurt.

Only now it looked like he'd just done it all over again.

"It won't happen again."

He watched silently as she ran her hands through her hair and took several deep breaths. "I'm going to head home. It's been a long day, and here I am taking it out on you. I'm sorry."

"You're not. You have nothing to be sorry for. This was on me. All of it."

"It's okay." She put her hand on the doorknob. "I'll feel better after a good night's sleep. We both will. See you in the morning?"

"Sure."

With that, she left the room. Seb stood there for a long moment and looked at the door that was now shut tight and thought how appropriate that seemed. Just when he'd been starting to think that maybe there was still a spark between them, he realized he was standing over a pile of cold, dead ashes instead.

And as hard as it was to face, he needed to acknowledge that Bella did not want him.

Not right now, and if he took her words at face value—and there was no reason not to—she didn't want him ever again. Not in that way. As the father of her children, yes. As a support system during the pregnancy, yes. But as a husband, lover and friend…no.

God, as a doctor, he'd had to give plenty of families pretty hopeless news about their loved ones before. But the one thing he'd never had to do was give equally hopeless news to himself. About someone he loved. About someone he would probably always love.

That was the biggest kick to the gut he'd ever had to face.

This time, Bella was earlier to arrive at the maternity clinic than Seb. She'd barely seen him the rest of the week. That was probably his doing. She knew she'd overreacted to that kiss, but she'd been really tired and emotionally vulnerable. When he'd stood in that hallway massaging her temples exactly like he'd done in times past, she'd closed her eyes, lost in a special kind of bliss that had hung on through him taking her blood pressure, to him brushing her cheeks with that sweet gentle touch of his that had made her senses ignite with a desperate need. A need that made her weak in the knees. And when he'd actually leaned down to kiss her… She'd been lost. Not in the past, but in hopes of the present. It was as if everything that they'd once meant to each other had rushed forward to that very moment. She'd been drowning in him. Drowning in the force of her need for him. If they hadn't been interrupted, he could have made love to her in that very room. And, *Dios*, what a mistake that would have been.

One that would have been hard to find her way back from.

Maybe he wasn't even coming today. The thought should have filled her with relief, but instead it spurred a dread so great that she almost couldn't catch her breath. It was as if a huge band was tightening around her chest and constricting her lungs.

Then the bell over the door sounded, and her head whipped around to see who it was.

Seb. He'd come after all.

Afraid he'd see everything written on her face, she gave a quick wave and then bowed her head to stare sightlessly at her notebook of names. Tonight they still had to face his parents for dinner and pretend everything was okay when it wasn't. When it hadn't been for a long time.

He sat down next to her. "Hey."

She couldn't help her smile as she returned the greeting. It was another old habit of theirs, and one that was evidently just as hard to break just like so many other things. Like her reactions to his touch.

There were several other people in the waiting room, so she kept her voice low. "I'm really sorry about the other night. I know I overreacted and—"

"No, you were right. It's okay. Let's just forget it and move on."

Forget it and move on? Could they really do that?

Maybe he could, but Bella had a harder time with having hope waved in front of her heart only to have it yanked away again with a taunting *na-na-na-na-boo-boo.*

Even though he hadn't said the words in a malicious way, it still sliced her open all over again. And honestly, it wasn't fair of her to cast him as the villain when she'd been the one to tell him not to kiss her again.

She decided to change the subject, keeping her head close to his. "What do you want to do about your parents?"

"I think we should cancel."

This time she looked at his face. "Seb, why?"

"I really don't want to explain what's going on with us right now, because I don't really have a good handle on where we're going to end up, and if she senses something's wrong, she's going to ask. She's not afraid of confrontation, and she does it well. You know that as well as I do."

He was right. She did. But only because she was forthright and didn't like to play games. Like the one she and Seb were playing right now? Playing house, when neither one of them wanted to be there.

Well, she did. A little too much. And that's what had scared her about that kiss. Because she wanted it to be real. She wanted it to be about her and not just about the babies, and she was terrified that that's all it would ever be at this point.

Muscle memory was evidently a powerful thing. How long before those neural pathways could be rerouted to a healthier place?

"We need to tell her about the babies, Seb. The longer we wait, the more betrayed she's going to feel, especially if she finds out the people at the hospital knew before she did."

He paused. "You're absolutely right. The longer we wait, the more betrayed she's going to feel."

Like he'd felt, when she'd kept the truth from him?

"We don't have to tell her we're not together anymore in the sense of husband and wife. Can't that wait until later? Until after the babies are born?"

They were called back before Seb had a chance to answer. Her nerves were a mess, and when they took her blood pressure, they found it was still a little elevated. But this time there was a good reason for it. She was afraid he was thinking about moving out before the babies were even born. Maybe that was the smarter path…the rerouting neural synapses path, but right now she couldn't face walking around that apartment by herself. It would remind her how horrible it had been to live there alone when Seb had gone to Africa. How the hallways had seemed to echo with memories that couldn't be erased.

She could probably face that after the babies were born. She could sell the place, or just hand it over to Seb and find another apartment for herself and the babies. But would it be any better? Would she still long for his presence in her life?

Was this how her mom had felt looking at the prospect of being a single mom? Of being the one to put her child to bed night after night without the support of someone who loved her? At least until she married the man who Bella thought of as her dad.

She smiled at Jessica as she came into the room. "Okay, we're at almost nineteen weeks, it looks like."

Today her hair was caught up in a clip that did nothing to blot out the picture that this was a woman who was not only a free spirit but also at peace with the world.

Bella felt anything but peaceful.

She found herself letting Seb do most of the talking; she was just not in a place where she could chitchat, although she did manage to tell Jessica the names they'd chosen. She couldn't stop thinking about his parents. Seb's dad had had leukemia; did she really want to break the news to him that she and Seb were probably going to split up?

She didn't. But she also didn't know how they were going to keep it from them. Maybe Seb could talk to his mom privately and let her know that things weren't good in their relationship but ask her to keep it from her husband for now.

That seemed just as bad as pretending to be a happy couple when they weren't.

Bella got onto the table and lay back, preparing for the ultrasound. This time, Seb didn't help her adjust her clothes, and she found she missed the easy way he'd done that last time.

Muscle memory. It'll fade with time.

And even though he moved to stand beside her, he made no attempt to hold her hand as Jessica waved her magic wand over Bella's abdomen as if casting a spell on the babies inside of it.

Baby C, please come out this time.

She studied the images trying to see what Jessica did, although she wasn't an ob-gyn.

"Do you want to know the gender?"

"Can you tell?" Seb asked the question.

"I'm pretty sure. Baby C is cooperating a little more this morning and doesn't have his butt to us."

Bella looked up at Seb. "I want to know. You?"

"Yes. I do as well."

Jessica turned back to the screen. "Okay…

so, names. We have Sergio, Lorenzo and Luis picked out for the boys, right?"

"Yes. Wait. Does that mean they're boys? All three of them?"

Jessica laughed. "That's what I'm saying, although ultrasounds aren't a perfect science. Any specific baby you want to assign those names to?"

"Oh, Seb. We have baby boys." Bella's eyes filled with tears and she couldn't stop herself from holding out her hand, praying Seb would take it. He did, giving it a light squeeze, but he didn't let it go, like she'd halfway expected him to. And although his grip wasn't as tight as it had been the last time they'd been in this room, it didn't feel totally apathetic either. But when she looked up at him, she saw she wasn't the only one who was moved with emotion. Seb's jaw was tight as if fighting his own feelings.

They stared at the screen. The babies were in much the same order as they were the last time, except Baby C had separated himself a little more. She still couldn't see his chest or head, but he was there.

She wanted Seb to name them. She squeezed his hand. "You decide."

"Let's do them in the order you said earlier, Jessica. Sergio, Lorenzo and little Luis. Does that work?"

"It does." Bella looked closer and saw he was right. "Is it my imagination or is Luis smaller than the other two? Or is it just because there's not as much of him visible?"

Jessica was concentrating on something and didn't say anything for a minute before turning her attention back to them. "Yes, he does appear to be smaller, but he might still catch up. Or he might stay little. I actually would like you to come back again in a week or two. Something is bothering me."

"About the babies?" Fear threatened to clog her throat.

"No, just about the fact that I still can't see Luiz completely. Especially on multiples, I really want to look for congenital problems so we're ready for them when it comes time to deliver them. I'm not expecting to find anything, but I'd like to be able to mark that off my punch list."

Bella felt better. She often had a punch list of her own when patients came in, sorting through various diagnoses and marking some as possibilities and ruling others out completely.

"Do the other two look okay?" Seb asked.

"Yes, from what I can tell, Sergio and Lorenzo are perfect. And what I can see of Luis is good as well—half of his spine and abdomen are visible and look okay, but just to put all of our minds at ease, I'd like to get a peek at the rest of him."

"That makes sense to me," Bella said, glancing up at Seb again. "Are you available again next week?"

"Yes. Whatever we can do to make sure everything is okay with them." He glanced at the screen. "Can you write their names on the sonogram for me?"

It might seem like a funny request, but she understood why he'd made it. He was already visualizing them as little people, just as she was. It made them all the more real. Bella pictured Seb talking to the triplets through her belly, and her jaw tightened. Would he do that? Did she even want him to do that? The intimacy of him murmuring to his babies was something she'd once dreamed of.

She did want him to. Whether or not they ever got back together, it would mean the world to their kids that he'd interacted with them when they'd still been inside of her. Her own father hadn't, her mom had told her. She hadn't wanted him to, since they weren't together. And maybe that had been the right decision for her mother, but Bella didn't think it was the right decision for her. She and Seb had been very much in love when they'd gotten married. And she wanted him to know his children as intimately as she was coming to know them. That meant she wanted him at every screening, at every sonogram, at every doctor's appointment, or at least as many as he could manage.

She certainly wouldn't stop him from doing any of those things. If he wanted to be there for the birth, if he wanted to coach her through it, she would welcome it. All of it. She might be afraid for him to kiss her, but she yearned for his participation in the babies' birth stories.

Jessica was busy replacing the letters for each baby with his name. Once she was done, she printed off a copy and handed it to her. Bella couldn't contain her smile.

"Sergio, Lorenzo and Luis, welcome to our family."

She only realized she'd said the words aloud when Seb leaned down to softly kiss her bare belly. It was a mere touch, and then it was gone, but it sent a shock wave through her that went straight down to her toes. It also sent a streak of joy tearing through her heart. They might not make it through this as a couple, but she had no doubt that these babies would be ridiculously loved. By both of them.

She reached up and touched his face. "Thanks for being here for this. For all of it."

"You're welcome."

Armed with their paper and released by Jessica to go back into the world with a good report so far on the babies' health, they walked out of the clinic.

"We can make a copy of this for your folks, if you want."

"That's kind of why I wanted her to put their names on it." He stopped her before they reached the parking lot. "My parents obviously don't know we're having problems, and the last thing I want to do is pretend to be a happy couple tonight if you're not up to it, but I do want to have our stories straight before we get there."

She thought for a minute. "I don't want to hurt your parents. And I also don't want to lie to them. But the truth is, even we don't know where we'll be in a year. In two years. So why don't we just approach it that way? We're certainly civil to each other, and we've proven we can hold hands without any animosity toward one another, so why don't we do that? We'll hold hands and smile at each other. The stuff we did in that exam room a few minutes ago. I think your mom will be so ecstatic over the news she's finally going to have grandchildren that I don't think she'll be looking for signs of a ruined marriage."

"Is that what we have? A ruined marriage?"

"I honestly don't know, Seb. But I don't think that's something we have to sort out at this exact moment. Maybe it's like Luis. We can't see all that's there or not there right now. We just have to wait for things to reveal themselves and then go from there."

He smiled at her and this time, it was a genuine smile that reached his eyes and every other part of his face. "Wise words from a wise woman."

He put his hand on her stomach. "Did you hear that, boys?" Then he looked at her. "And thanks for being willing to go with me to break the news to my parents."

"I'm happy to." Right now, it was the truth. She felt happy and if not exactly hopeful, she didn't feel as hopeless as she had when that kiss had ended in the exam room.

Maybe she was carving some new neural

pathways after all. And not all of them were doom and gloom. For her sake and the sake of the babies, those were the ones she was going to start nurturing in the hope that something good could still come from all the heartache of the past.

CHAPTER SEVEN

INSTEAD OF GOING back to the apartment, they'd gone to the park instead and moseyed their way through it, taking Jessica's admonition to heart about getting out in the fresh air and walking. They'd talked about his parents and even about Seb's time in Africa. She'd been moved to tears over his recounting of a couple of the stories about the conditions some of the people faced. Conditions that were faced in almost every country of the world, including Argentina. Hunger, fear, disease. They were things that spoke of the human condition.

Just like Mario, their electrocution patient who was still in ICU, but whose heart was still beating, whose brain was still functioning, even if his hands never would again. They'd both had to be amputated to save his life. His wife was just so grateful that he was alive that it didn't matter that he'd no longer be able to do a lot of things. But he'd still be able to make a living as a shop owner in a poor neighborhood. At least with some help. And he could help educate others about the dangers of trying to hook into the city's power grid without being detected. Sometimes it worked...but when it didn't, people lost their lives.

They didn't rent a paddleboat this time; instead they stuck to the shady paths and wandered with no definite direction in mind. The day wasn't quite as hot as it had been yesterday, and the park was magical. The sounds of the water, the happiness of kids running along the paths, the birds that sang in the trees. Seb didn't reach for her hand, but he felt connected to her in a way he hadn't in a long time. Maybe it was due to naming the babies, but he had a feeling it was more than that.

And when Bella asked to rest on a bench for a while, he sat next to her. Not talking, just sitting there and letting time tick by. For once it didn't seem to be rushing at a frenetic pace waiting for him to catch up with it. It was just crawling leisurely by and, for once, Seb was happy to just be there in the moment. Especially since he didn't know how many more of them he would get.

The doctor was right. They needed to come here more often and just enjoy each other's company. If not as lovers, then maybe they could manage it as friends.

"Are we ready for tonight?" she said.

"I'm not sure I'm ever fully ready for a night with my parents."

She smiled. "It won't be that bad. I love your mom and dad."

"I love them, too. My mom can just be a bit *exigente* sometimes."

"I think all parents can be that way. She just wants to see you happy."

He didn't exactly have a response for that comment, so he sat back and watched a bird hop by looking for small bits of food. "If we can get through tonight, we should be good."

Did he really believe that? His parents would be crushed when he and Bella eventually separated. But then again, they couldn't stay together just for that reason. Or for the babies. Fate had a way of making you resent not having the life you envisioned. Or being stuck in a life you don't exactly want.

With him and Bella, though, it was tricky. Because he was pretty sure neither of them knew which category they fell into. She—and her doctor—wanted him there to help her during the pregnancy, but he was pretty sure for Bella, it didn't go beyond that, if her words after that kiss were anything to go by. And he couldn't blame her. How did you tell someone you were done without telling them you're done? You do exactly what Seb did and leave for months. He'd come back to Argentina expecting to call it quits, only to find he wasn't as sure as he'd thought he was. But it seemed Bella believed in the mantra that actions speak louder than words. And his actions had done their job and more.

Trying to shake off his morose thoughts, he glanced over at her to find her hands were both on her belly and there was a strange look on her face. "What is it?"

"I think I felt them. There was some quivery little sensation a minute ago. It's gone now, but… After the ultrasound and the names, it just feels so real all of a sudden."

"It is real, Bella." This was all happening so fast. In less than three weeks since he'd come home, he'd found out Bella was expecting, he'd been to three doctor's appointments, had picked out baby names, and had heard and seen his babies via ultrasound. If he remembered his medical training correctly, then by week twenty he'd be able to feel the baby's kicks, too, by putting his hands on Bella's stomach. No wonder he felt like his world was spinning.

"I know, but…" She glanced his way. "I'm glad you're here for it."

"I'm glad I am, too." Her words made his gut tighten, but he had to remember that what she said and what he heard were probably two different things. She was glad he was here for the pregnancy. But was she glad he was here for her personally? If he'd come home and she hadn't been pregnant, would she have kicked him to the curb? He wouldn't have blamed her if she had.

He told himself it could be worse. She could have been pregnant and still kicked him to the curb, and he would have deserved it. Instead, here she was sharing the experience with him.

He decided to ask a question that had been circling in his head for a while. "Do you want me there with you for the actual birth?"

She blinked. "Do you want to be there for the birth?"

He smiled. "We could go back and forth answering your question with a question forever. The truth is, I want to be there, but only if you want me there. Only if it helps you get through the experience. I don't want to do anything that makes the process harder for you than it needs to be."

"I want you there."

"Then I'll be there." And since he'd already voiced the first question, he decided to ask the second one he'd been fretting over. "How late in the pregnancy are you planning to work?"

"Until I'm told not to by my doctor." She twisted her hands together. "I know you're worried, but right now I can't just sit at home. I'll drive myself crazy by overthinking things too much."

He tried to put himself in her shoes. He would probably do the same thing. Sit there and stew about things that he could do nothing about. He did enough of that as it was. But he had a thought.

"What if you still went to work, but you did more paperwork for the department and I spent more time on the floor?"

"You mean reverse our usual roles?" She shook her head. "It would never work. Mainly because I don't like paperwork."

Okay, so much for that idea. "How about this, then. How about if I ask for our schedules to line up and when you get tired, you can go to the office. The upshot is, I'll spend more time in the ER doing actually emergency care than I've been doing."

"But the paperwork needs to get done, too."

"And it will get done. By me, or I can ask the hospital administrator for a medical student who's looking for some hospital experience to be assigned to the ER. They could get some actual floor time while coming on board to learn the paperwork side of things."

"That sounds doable. But if they say no, then I don't want you killing yourself trying to get the other stuff done after your shift ends."

"I won't. But in the same vein, I don't want you running yourself to exhaustion trying to take up the slack for everyone else. When you're short-staffed it needs to be a shared load, agreed?"

"Agreed."

"That means actually picking up your phone and calling me and telling me to get my backside on the floor."

She laughed. "You want me to say it exactly like that? Because people might wonder what I am trying to get you to do."

Suddenly an image that had nothing to do with him going to the ER flickered across his mental movie screen.

"Okay, well maybe just say, 'I need you on the floor.'" As soon as he said the words he realized it wasn't any better. If anything, it was worse.

"Yeah… I don't think I'm going to be calling our office anytime soon."

But at least she was smiling.

"Just call and say you're tired. I'll get the message."

She glanced at her watch, a smile still on her face. "Speaking of tired. We have a little bit of a hike to get back to the parking lot, and I probably should get home so I can change before we head over to your folks' house."

"Are you sure you want to do this?"

She reached over and grabbed his hand. "Seb. We've been over this several times. Yes, we should go. And yes, I'll be okay. You have to trust me on this one."

"Okay." With that they got up and started the long walk back to the park's entrance. He smiled. He could say, for once, that today was a good day.

Bella positively glowed, and he'd never been more proud of her than he was at that moment. She'd dressed in a loose summer dress that didn't immediately reveal her condition, and she looked cool and beautiful as she kissed his mom and dad with genuine affection and handed over the bottle of wine they'd brought. "It's so good to see you again. Thanks for having us."

"Anytime, Bella. I'm sorry we didn't get together more while Seb was away. I dropped the ball on that," his mom said apologetically.

"No. You didn't. You did try, but I was either working or at my mom's house helping her with something so if anything, it was more my fault."

"Well, Seb is back and you're here now, and that's all that matters." She turned and gave Seb a kiss as well. "Now come and sit down and tell us everything about your trip. I'm just putting dinner on the table."

They sat down to eat, and he told some of the same stories from Angola that he'd shared with Bella. But as much as he'd enjoyed talking about it earlier, telling them to his parents raised feelings of guilt all over again. Not just for leaving Bella, but leaving his parents, especially his dad. What if something had happened to him when he'd been so far away? He finally stopped mid-sentence and decided to just rip off the Band-Aid.

"Mom and Dad, we have some news we

want to share with you." He stopped again as a wave of emotion washed up his throat and threatened to choke him.

Bella came to the rescue, covering his hand with hers. "We should have told you sooner, but it was something Seb and I wanted to do together, after he came home from his assignment overseas."

"What is it, dear?"

Bella smiled. "Actually…we're expecting. I'm pregnant."

He still hadn't figured out exactly how he was going to explain the delay in sharing the news, but Bella had come up with the perfect answer.

And from his mom's shriek, it had been exactly the right one. "You're pregnant?" She came around the table and hugged Bella and then returned to her seat and embraced her husband for a long moment. When she turned back to them, her eyes were glistening with tears. "We're going to be grandparents?"

Seb nodded. "You are."

Reaching into her tote bag, Bella pulled out the sonogram with the boys' names on it and handed it to them.

His mom looked up. "Wait. What's this? Three names? Are you trying to choose one?"

Her eyes widened. "One of these is your father's name."

Seb smiled. "I know that, and no, we don't need to choose one. We've already chosen them."

"You mean…"

"Yes, we're having triplets."

"*Dios mio.* Are you telling me the truth?" This time she looked at Bella, maybe thinking she was going to say it was all one big joke. Except it wasn't.

"I swear we are. We are having three boys. Depending on how many embryos are implanted, some of them take and some don't. My doctor implanted three, but because of how carefully she chose them, they all took. And I opted to carry all three."

"You both must be over the moon. I know I am. After all this time." She glanced at her husband. "It's unbelievable. When are they due?"

Seb responded. "We don't exactly know. Because of the risks, our doctor has said she would feel better doing a cesarean, so it's doubtful that they'll go all the way to nine months. They'll probably take them out a few weeks early."

"Yes, whatever is safer for Bella and the babies." She clapped her hands together. "You've both made me happier than you can imagine. All I ever wanted was for my only child to be happy and to make me a grandmother."

Little did she know that she'd almost gotten neither of those things. If the pregnancy hadn't taken and he'd stuck to his guns, she wouldn't be a grandmother at all. And her only child would probably be in the middle of a divorce right now and not happy at all. Seb might have asked Bella a couple of hard questions at the park, but he hadn't asked her the hardest one of all: What did she intend to do about their marriage after the babies were born?

Seb forced a smile. "I'm glad you're so happy."

"We must go shopping for clothes for you and the babies and..."

This time his dad stopped her. "Take a few breaths, dear. I can't keep up with you, and I'm not even pregnant."

"Dad's right," Seb said. "Bella has been feeling a little tired recently, and so I'm trying to get her to agree to slow down the pace."

"How far along are you?"

"Getting close to nineteen weeks," Bella said.

Here was the moment of truth. Either his

mom would be upset that she was so late to the game, or she would accept it and move on. He hoped for the latter.

"Yes, I remember I felt really good in my second trimester, but I still tired out pretty easily."

Thanks, Mom. He sent the words up into the universe.

Thankfully she didn't ask very many more questions, she just rattled off sentence after sentence in a long stream-of-consciousness monologue that made him both cringe and smile. She really was one of a kind. Yet today had gone so much better than it could have. Seb tended to lean toward worst-case scenario, and it was always a relief when it didn't come to pass.

When he was finally able to get a word in edgewise, he looked at his dad. "What have you been up to lately?"

"Well, I actually retired last week."

"What?"

His mom had the grace to look embarrassed. "That's right. I got so caught up in the news about the babies, I forgot to share some news of our own. We're going to start doing some traveling. You're not the only one with itchy feet."

That took him aback. She'd never once mentioned wanting to travel. He glanced quickly at his dad, who caught the look.

"Don't worry. I'm fine. I've been wanting to go to Scotland for a while, and I finally talked your mom into it. I figured I had one shot at this, and I'd better make it something she's interested in doing as well."

"But with the babies on the way maybe we should rethink…" His mom started to say something before letting the sentence fade away.

Seb broke in. "The babies won't be here for a while, and even after they arrive you don't have to sit at home just because of them. We'll make sure you have plenty of opportunities to be with them."

Too late he realized he'd spoken for Bella, too, in his sentence, but when he looked over at him she smiled and gave his hand a squeeze. "Yes, we will. My grandparents meant an awful lot to me, and I want our babies to get to spend time with theirs on both sides as well. My mom and dad are over the moon, too."

His mom's forehead furrowed just a tiny bit, and he knew something about what Bella had said had caught her attention. But the expression cleared so quickly he wasn't sure he'd even seen it. "Well, I made *flan de naranja* for dessert."

His mom's baked orange flan was delicious and was another one of Bella's favorite dishes. He had no doubt she'd made it just for her.

"Yum, thank you so much."

"You're welcome. And there's no alcohol in it. Seb didn't say anything, but he hesitated for a minute over the wine, so I wondered if you were still trying to get pregnant. But I had no idea you'd succeeded." She reached over the table and took one of Bella's hands. "I'm so glad, Bella. You two have been trying for so long."

Bella was very still, and he wondered if she was thinking the same thing that he was. If this attempt hadn't worked, Seb's adamant refusal to try again would have kept her from ever having children.

Not for the first time, he wondered if he'd been wrong in deciding something for the both of them. And in reality, she could have divorced him and tried again with donor sperm. But the guilt about leaving wasn't just about that. It was about making a unilateral decision for someone else. He wasn't sure he'd been right at all when he looked at it like that. And yet there was no way for him to have known that there was a possibility of coming out on the other side with a viable pregnancy. Not after all their other failures.

When there was continued silence, he said, "But this time it did. So we're very happy about that."

"Yes, we are."

Soon the talk changed from pregnancy to his parents' travel plans, which they talked about over dessert. There was plenty of laughter as his dad's dry sense of humor finally had a chance to come out and play. He joked that he was kilt shopping and wanted to know who wanted to go with him.

Seb rolled his eyes. "And on that note, I think we're going to take off." Although Bella was still laughing and actively involved in the conversation, it had been a long day for her, and he was sure she had to be running out of steam. He knew he was.

Not to mention his parents lived on the outskirts of Buenos Aires, so they still had almost an hour-long drive back to their apartment.

They stood up and embraced his folks once

again and took the proffered tubs of leftovers that his mom insisted they have.

So with arms full, they headed back to their car.

Once everything was loaded, he opened Bella's door for her and then got in on his side of the vehicle. She turned to him with a smile. "Well, that went better than I thought it would."

"Thanks to you. That was quick thinking about mentioning us wanting to tell them together."

"It was the truth, actually. Why do you think I avoided meeting her for coffee? I didn't want to have to go back and explain why I hadn't told her about the pregnancy over a coffee date."

He touched her face, again marveling how soft her skin was. "Thank you so much for being willing to come with me and take them on."

"It wasn't a problem at all. And I'm really glad your dad is going to take some time and do the things he's wanted to do."

"Me, too. I was halfway worried that his cancer might have come back, but I don't think that's what was behind the travel bug.

I truly think he just wants to do some of the things he never got to do while working."

"Your mom was happy about the babies, I think."

"Happy? I think that's an understatement."

He started the car and headed back to the city, glancing over at her a couple of times and finding her dozing in her seat. She'd seemed genuinely at ease tonight. Putting on some soft music to drown out some of the noise of horns honking and general traffic sounds, he hoped she could sleep the rest of the way home. She needed it.

But what did he need?

Her. He needed her, like he always had. He just hadn't been able to see through the grief and the mire that made up their attempts at getting pregnant. If the initial fertility treatment had worked, would they have found themselves in the situation they were now in?

There was no way to know. No way to go back and see how that particular future would have unrolled. If he could travel back in time, would he have wanted to stop their attempts sooner? Probably. The last couple of cycles, he'd only done it for Bella in hopes that something would take. But it never had.

At least not until he'd been ready to give up completely.

Coming out on this side of things and knowing it was probably partly due to the fact that the last embryo transfer had worked, he only knew that he didn't want to lose her. Not now. Not after all these years of being together.

He was surprised when he turned down their road, realizing he'd driven most of the way on autopilot.

The way he'd been going through the last couple of years of his marriage?

Maybe it was time to change that. Maybe he wasn't as powerless as he'd thought he was. He could woo her and see where that got him. And if she had the same reaction that she'd had to that kiss? Well, then he'd have his answer. But if he just let her go without even trying to see if she still had any feelings for him, he would always wonder, and it would plague him for years to come.

He turned off the car and went around to the other side, opening the door and reaching over to undo her seat belt just as she stirred. She gazed up at him with glazed eyes.

"You fell asleep," he murmured. Ignoring the box of food on the back seat, he started to swing her up into his arms only to have her stop him.

"It's okay. I can walk. Plus there's all the stuff in the back seat to bring."

"Are you sure? I can come back and get it."

"I'm fine, really." She swung her legs out of the car and stood, yawning, but looking better than she had in a week. Which was surprising since she'd looked so exhausted at work the last couple of days. But maybe seeing his parents and getting the news off her chest had helped her. It certainly had him.

It could be that's where all these thoughts of trying to reconcile were coming from. They'd had a good time tonight at the park and at his parents. Couldn't they build on that?

He reached into the back seat and took out the boxes that held their food and walked with her to the elevator.

"Today was fun, wasn't it?"

"I was actually just thinking that, too."

She looked up at him in surprise. "You were?"

"Yep." He didn't want to share any more for fear of scaring her off, but decided to try to play it cool. "I think the doctor was right about getting out in the fresh air and enjoying some outings."

"I think we said the same thing on the paddleboat that first time."

"So we did."

He pushed the button in the elevator, and the car started its ascent. "Do you remember that time when that swan chased us halfway us up the bank of the lake and followed us onto the path?"

She laughed. "Yes, you'd tossed it part of a sandwich and it decided it wanted more. Except we didn't have any more, and the thing was mad."

"It actually ripped a hole in my shirt."

She bumped against his shoulder the way that she used to. "I remember. I also remember it was a new one and you were pretty ticked off."

"I remember. I also remember what happened later. When we reached the car."

"So do I. We didn't actually make it home. We had to stop halfway and park in a secluded spot."

"If we hadn't I would have crashed the car into a tree or something."

"You were so cute." The door to the elevator opened. "And it was so hot to watch you squirm."

They'd taken the long way home down back

roads, and Bella had licked and bitten at his neck as they drove, putting his hormones on high alert. Things had taken another turn when she'd slid his shirt up enough that she could splay her hand out over his abs. "What do you want, Seb?" she'd asked him.

"You, I want you."

They'd found a place behind a stand of trees and had consummated their love for each other. Even now he could feel her around him, taste her lips.

They got off the elevator and made it as far as the door. "Everything about that day was steamy, and not just because it was a hot day weather-wise."

"It was, wasn't it?" Bella leaned her back against the door to look up at him from under her eyelashes. "We were so carefree back then. We had so much fun. The park today reminded me of that day."

Seb had his keys in his hand, but he wasn't looking at the door. His attention was wholly fastened on the woman who was bringing up memories that he'd almost forgotten. Or maybe he'd forced himself to forget them. Although he had no idea how. Because right now he wanted her with a force that was almost overpowering. He wanted to relive a few of those steamy moments from the past.

"Bella..."

She reached up and cupped her face. "It's okay, Seb. We're not in a car right now. There's no danger of crashing into anything but each other." She slid her hand under his shirt, pressing her palm to his skin very much like she'd done back then.

And he came undone. His free arm went around her back and hauled her up against him for a moment, only to realize he needed it to unlock the door. When he finally got it open, he almost fell inside with her. With that he slammed the door, put the tubs of food on the nearby hall table, and put his mouth to hers.

CHAPTER EIGHT

BELLA WASN'T SURE why she'd brought up any of those memories, but the second his mouth came down on hers, she fell down a rabbit hole and found herself in another world. One she'd almost convinced herself hadn't ever really existed.

But there was nothing else like Seb's kiss. Even in those horrible days of IVF attempts, his lips against hers had always had the power to make her forget what they were hoping for. Then things had become overly cautious. And safe. It was like something, some special element, had been taken away from their relationship.

But she didn't have to be safe right now. At least not in the ways she was thinking.

She needed him. Right now. However she could get him. After all, Dr. Lucas had reassured them that sex was still on the table for now.

Reaching down, she unzipped his pants, freeing him.

"Wait, Bella, wait."

But she didn't want to wait. There was no need for condoms anymore. No need for anything "safe." She knew she needed to be careful of the pregnancy, but maybe one of their biggest failures back then had been in not experimenting with other ways to keep the mystery and passion alive.

And right now, she needed something that had some risk to it—not physical risk, because she'd never harm her babies, but emotional. Spinning him so that she again had her back to the door, she walked him over to the couch and pushed him down onto it, standing over him for a minute. She wasn't the only one who needed something, judging from the look of him.

And she'd always liked looking at him.

The day he'd come out of the shower, she hadn't been able to take her eyes off him. She'd wanted to touch him so very badly—and now she could.

She took a step closer and knelt in front of him, sliding her fingertips over his warm, firm flesh and relishing every time it jumped under her touch. "I'm so tired of playing it safe, Seb."

He chuckled. "One thing you've never been good at, if I remember right."

"Oh, really? I can be plenty safe." With that, she leaned over and kissed the flesh she'd been caressing.

She heard the hiss of air that said she'd shocked him with her sudden touch. But he didn't stop her as she tasted and nibbled her way over his skin. And when she finally enveloped him, she felt his hand on the back of her head. Not pushing or urging, but just threading itself through the strands of her hair as she picked up the pace.

"Bella… *Dios*…it's too much."

He hauled her off him and lifted her onto the couch so that she was straddling him. Her skirt was bunched between strong hands and pulled up until the backs of her bare thighs were against his jeans. He again buried his hand in her hair and kissed her, holding her tight against his mouth while his tongue thrust deep. This time it was Bella who squirmed, needing him so badly. But before she could lift herself up onto him, he stood, taking her with him, one hand sliding under her butt as he walked toward the bedroom they'd once shared.

God, she couldn't wait to share it with him again. For tonight at least. She would worry about tomorrow when it came.

The curve of her belly was pressed tight against his flat abs as she leaned down to kiss him again, her hair falling around them, making her wonder how he could even see. But evidently he could since he walked without hesitation to her bed, laying her oh so carefully on top of the covers. Something about that tickled at the back of her brain, but right now, she didn't care. She was frantic. Frantic to be with him. Frantic to touch him. Frantic for him to push her off that very sexy cliff the way he always used to.

Her skirt was still at the top of her thighs and with a secret smile, his palms slid up her skin and reached her panties, fingers hooking over the elastic waistband and pulling them down. When they were off her legs, he tossed them to the side.

"Take off your shirt," she whispered.

He seemed to hesitate for a split second before he hauled it over his head and tossed it in the direction of her undergarment. "Your turn."

Leaning over her, he slid her shirt up her belly and somehow got it over her head. The bra came next. He covered her breasts with his hands and gently squeezed. But it was too little. She ached to feel his mouth on them pulling hard. Ached to feel him inside of her.

He kissed her again, moving his body so that he was lying beside her but not on top of her, his hand skimming down her chest, over her belly and then lower, until he touched her gently. The unexpected contact made her arch up, seeking him. Still kissing her, he obliged, using his fingers to touch her, caress her, the sensation so painfully familiar that she gasped, her fingers reaching for the back of his head to pull him closer, to kiss him deeper, even as he slid two fingers inside of her, mimicking what she wanted so badly. She used her feet to push up into him, lost in a sensation she hadn't felt in so very long. His thumb continued to stroke her, varying his pace so that she was never sure when to meet him. She strained wanting more, wanting *him*, not just his hand. But things in her head began to get cloudy as the sensations continued to take over, rational thought sliding to the back of the line as she continued to revel in kisses that drugged her, making her forget anything except what was happening. Her hand slid sideways seeking something, but she wasn't quite sure at this point if she had the willpower to try to find it. To give to him what he was giving her.

Then his pace quickened slightly although his strokes didn't go any deeper than they already were. When he lifted his head and looked down at her, her breath came in gasps as her hips frantically sought something that wasn't there. But release was coming whether she got what she wanted or not, so she pushed up one more time as she finally gave in and let the waves of pleasure sweep over her, calling out his name as he leaned down to kiss her again. He continued kissing her as she slowly came down from the mountaintop, her brain cells engaging one by one. When she could finally think, she frowned and went to reach for him, but he murmured for her to wait a few minutes.

Wait? For what?

She blinked. Maybe he wasn't done with her. Maybe he was just giving her a few minutes to catch her breath. Okay, that made more sense. They'd done that in the past.

He lay down beside her and she curled around him, waiting. But a sense of lethargy was stealing over her, weighty and snug, like a heavy blanket. He'd told her to wait for a few minutes. That she could do. Then they would go another round. And this time, she would do for him what he'd just done for her…and more.

In just a few minutes.

She snuggled closer and felt him stroke her hair, her temples, his index finger trailing down the bridge of her nose. His touch brought with it a sense of comfort. Of relaxation.

Sighing as he continued to skim his fingers over her, she let her eyes close for a second, opening them with a jerk. Then they slid shut again, and she gave in to the steady, slow motions as Seb seemed to hypnotize her and send her off to another place. One where everything was okay with the world.

Bella woke with a start to find the sun was shining through the blinds on her window. She was on her bed, but she was sideways somehow, and the light comforter had been pulled up from the bottom of the bed and covered her.

She moved and realized she was mostly naked, except for her skirt.

Last night came back to her in a rush and she was horrified. She'd fallen asleep on Seb before he'd gotten any satisfaction of his own. *Dios!* How could she have been so selfish? He'd given her everything and gotten nothing in return.

She turned to find him to make that right, except he wasn't in the bed. Her eyes swept the space, including the open door to the en suite. He wasn't in the room. At all. So where was he?

Looking at her watch, another wave of horror went through her. She'd somehow overslept and was now late for work. Seb would have to take a rain check on whatever he'd been planning for himself.

Except something tickled the back of her brain again, like it had last night. Surely he'd wanted to get something out of what they'd done together. What sort of person wouldn't?

So why hadn't he woken her up or stuck around until this morning? Maybe he had, and she'd simply slept on through the night. He'd talked about them starting to work the same shifts, so maybe he'd gone on into the hospital.

She jerked upright in the bed; the remembered pleasure from last night washed over her again, making her close her eyes. She'd thought this part of her life with Seb was gone for good. So for him to want to…

Wait. She'd started it, hadn't she? With her talk about the past and leaning against the door trying to look seductive. Had she really done that?

She had. And she'd been the one to unzip him and take him in her hands. To kiss him.

But he'd reciprocated, right? He had to have wanted it, too, or he would have pulled away…wouldn't he?

Right now things were so jumbled inside of her that she wasn't sure what was what. So she was going to get up and see if Seb was still here. If not, she was going to get dressed and head into work and try to figure out what exactly had happened last night. Maybe she even owed him an apology for falling asleep on him.

She wandered out into the main part of the apartment, not even bothering to get dressed, because the second she had opened the door she'd sensed he wasn't in the apartment.

So she went back into her bedroom and took a quick shower, trying to wash away all of the little prickles of unease that were beginning to cascade over her. Something just didn't feel right about last night. But the only way to know for sure was to find him and look into his face. If what she saw didn't satisfy her, she needed to ask him outright. No more guessing about what he thought or didn't think. No more guessing about where their relationship stood. Or didn't stand. Last night he'd finally given her hope that they might get past this.

So why hadn't he stayed to talk to her? Or at least left a note telling her where he'd gone and why?

Maybe he was angry with her about last night.

No, he hadn't seemed that way. He'd looked almost…at peace. She'd seen none of the desperation on his face that she'd felt for release. Had he climaxed while he was pleasuring her? She didn't think so. He'd seemed almost singular in his actions as if he knew exactly what he was doing. And why.

Then she'd just fallen asleep! She was pretty sure he hadn't planned for that.

Taking more care with her hair and makeup than she had in a while, she draped her lanyard over her neck and went into the kitchen to get a glass of milk. A bouquet of flowers sat in a vase of water on the bar. Her favorites. White daisies and pink roses. There was no note propped up, but it had to be from Seb, unless it was from his parents. No, they wouldn't know what flowers she liked best.

She leaned down to smell the sweet fragrance of the roses, allowing herself a slight smile. He wasn't mad at her, that much was certain. Maybe they could try again tonight, and this time she would be more insistent about his needs being met.

Feeling a little lighter, she flounced out the door in a fresh skirt and blouse and feeling on top of the world for the first time in a long time.

When she got to the hospital, she didn't see Seb on the floor, and so she went to the office to see if he was there. It was empty. Going over to the desk, she spotted a note he'd scribbled with the word *Jessica* on it along with a phone number. She frowned before realizing it was Dr. Lucas, the at-risk pregnancy specialist. He must have had a question about something, or maybe he was simply seeing when their next appointment was.

She shrugged and started to go out of the office when there was a knock on the door. "Come in."

A woman stood in the doorway. "Dr. Lopez?"

She got this a lot. "I'm Dr. Lopez, but I'm Isabella Lopez. Are you looking for me or my husband?"

She smiled. "I didn't realize there were two of you. I just came up to introduce myself."

The woman spoke Spanish, but it was accented. She was obviously not Argentine. It suddenly dawned on her who this might be. She'd forgotten her name when she'd talked to Seb about her earlier, but had looked it up later. "Are you Dr. Gonzalez, by any chance?"

She was supposed to meet with the other doctor at some point, but the administration hadn't nailed down a date for her, unless she'd missed a memo. What she really wanted to do was find Seb, but maybe it was better to let herself digest what had happened last night and think it over rather than rushing to him and blurting out everything she was thinking.

"I am. But please call me Emilia. Do you have a minute to talk?"

"Absolutely, come on in."

Emilia came the rest of the way into the office, and Bella motioned to the couch on the other side of the room. "Do you want some coffee? Water?"

"No. I'm okay." She perched on the front

of the sofa and waited for Bella to sit in one of the chairs across from her.

"You're a neonatal specialist, right? And you're from Uruguay?"

"I am," Emilia confirmed.

Bella tilted her head. "Do you have family in Argentina?"

"Not yet, but I will pretty soon. My daughter is getting ready to attend university, and she's gotten a scholarship to attend one here in Buenos Aires. As a mom, it's hard to just let her go off to another country on her own, so when I heard about the position opening here at the hospital, I jumped at it."

"How wonderful." Bella was happy for her, and since there was no mention of a father being in the picture, she assumed Emilia was going it on her own. She understood that all too well. If things didn't go well with Seb, she might very well be taking a similar path. "I get it. I'm actually pregnant with triplets right now."

"Wow, how far along?"

"Nineteen weeks."

The woman looked like she wanted to ask something else, but didn't, so Bella added a little more. "I've had several rounds of IVF, and it finally took after years of trying."

"I bet you and your husband are ecstatic."

This comment wasn't as easy to reply to. "I'd like to hope we both are."

"I'm happy for you." Emilia smiled. "I won't hold you up much longer. From your perspective, is there anything special I should know about the hospital?"

She thought for a minute. "It's a great place to work. And it's a popular medical center, so sometimes our schedules are pretty hectic. The neonatal unit is top-notch, so you'll get a lot of patients and doctors coming to you for advice."

"Which is great. I'd rather stay busy. It gives me less time to think."

About her daughter growing up and leaving the nest? That had to be it.

"It's really nice to meet you. If you ever have any questions, please don't hesitate to reach out to me or any of the other doctors. We're a pretty close-knit bunch."

"Thanks, and if you ever have any questions about your babies, please come find me."

"I absolutely will. Thank you." It was good to know that there'd be someone else at the hospital that she could reach out to if she had any concerns.

With that, Emilia stood up. "Well, like I

said, I won't keep you. I just wanted to meet you since the ER probably sees a lot of our patients before we do."

"Do you already have the job?"

"It's looking promising, so I'm hopeful."

"Good luck, and I'm serious about being available to answer any questions." Bella smiled and walked her to the door. "And if you find yourself with some spare time, let me know and we can go out for coffee…well, herbal tea in my case. But at least I can still enjoy the scent of coffee."

"I will. Thanks for letting me stop by."

"Any time." With that, the other woman stepped out of the office and headed for the elevator.

Bella liked her and made a mental note to seek her out and maybe take her to see some of the sights of the city.

As she started to shut the door, something stopped it from moving. Thinking it was the other doctor coming back to ask her something, she smiled and said, "Did you forget something?" as she opened the door.

Except it wasn't Emilia, it was Seb.

"Who were you talking to?"

"The neonatology candidate I told you about stopped by to introduce herself to us.

But you weren't here." She frowned. "You weren't at home, either. I looked for you."

He shifted from one foot to the other. "Sorry. You were sleeping so soundly, I didn't want to wake you."

"I noticed. You should have, though. I didn't want last night to be all about me. I hope you know that. I can't believe I fell asleep on you. All I can say is that I'm very sorry."

"Don't be. I was fine."

"Fine?" How could he be fine if he hadn't… "I don't understand."

Before he could answer, she glanced back at the desk and saw the slip of paper there. "Did you need to ask Jessica Lucas something? I saw her number on your desk."

This time he looked even more uncomfortable. She remembered asking for more last night, using her hips to try to get it, but he'd never penetrated her fully, even manually. "Did it have to do with last night?"

He gave a half shrug. "I wanted to make sure the babies couldn't be hurt by what we did."

The babies. He was concerned about the babies. Suddenly it all made sense. Even the fact that he'd been careful about handling her breasts, too. She remembered the doctor talking about not engaging in nipple stimulation, but that was toward the end of pregnancy.

Her eyes closed. "Jessica said that sex wasn't off the table. Not at this point."

"I know. But I just wanted to be sure."

"So why didn't you ask *me*? Do you think I would do something if it risked this pregnancy?" She suddenly felt like a fool. She'd practically begged him for more and had tried to reach out for him only to have him pull away. Just like he had when she'd thought the IVF had failed again.

Had he even wanted her at all last night? Or had he simply given in to what she wanted because she was the babies' mother?

She felt an initial rush of humiliation until she remembered he'd definitely been aroused. She was sure of it. But he hadn't acted on that arousal. She should have realized. Something hadn't felt right at the time, but as usual she'd pushed until she got her way and now… And now she was faced with the realization that he probably wouldn't have started anything with her on his own. He'd certainly made it plain enough when he'd said about waiting a little while. He knew her well enough to know that she often fell asleep in his arms after reaching her release. And he'd purposely coaxed her into heading in that direction. She squirmed, humiliation washing over her again.

"Don't bother calling Jessica and asking. There's no need, because I don't see this happening again in the foreseeable future."

"Bella..."

She held up a hand. "No, please don't. I think you were right all along. You said we needed some time apart before you left for Africa. *When I thought I was losing the pregnancy.*"

She knew the bitterness in her voice was coming through loud and clear, but she couldn't seem to stanch the flow. It was like he'd nicked an emotional artery, and now every single hurt that she'd felt over the last couple of years was pouring out.

"You'll be happy to know I finally agree with you. We need some time. *I* need some time. You've offered to do my shift for me, so today, have at it. I'm going to go back to the apartment and figure out where *I* need to go from here."

Before he had a chance to say anything else, she whirled around and left the office, not even saying goodbye. Because when she did say it, it was going to be for good.

Except she knew in her heart of hearts that

there was nothing good about a final goodbye. There was only pain and heartbreak. But right now, she couldn't see any way around that. For either of them.

CHAPTER NINE

BELLA GOT HOME and threw herself on the bed, sobbing until she had no more tears inside of her to cry. She pulled the comforter around her, chilled and sad, thinking that nothing seemed to make sense. In all the time that he'd been in the apartment, it felt as though everything had been about the babies or the pregnancy.

It hurt like hell that he'd thought she would do something so unconsidered, so rash, to harm them. She was very aware that they were his children, too.

So why did she have to beg for everything? She'd begged last night in much the same way she'd begged him to be willing to try again before he'd left for Africa. It was so hard to believe that had been only a few short months ago.

Did she want Seb to go? To end their marriage?

Another sob escaped her throat, and she had to steel herself not to fall apart all over again. She didn't want him to leave. But he couldn't stay, either. Not with the way things were between them right now. She did not want someone in her life who was only there for the children. It would be too hard. Because she wanted Seb, and for her that part had nothing to do with the kids, even if it might have seemed like it at the time.

So what did she do? Talk to him again? Every time she tried to do that, things went sideways.

Maybe. Maybe like she'd begged him to do all those months ago, she should ask for another chance. Not for the babies, but for their relationship.

She just wasn't sure she had the courage to. Not anymore.

But lying here on the bed feeling sorry for herself was helping nothing, either.

She cranked herself upright and took stock of the situation, going into the kitchen for another glass of milk.

She'd cried so hard that she felt completely empty, her stomach muscles sore. The flowers were still on the bar, seeming to mock her tears. She understood his need to keep the peace, and maybe he'd felt guilty over last night.

Calling Jessica may have been his way of making sure he hadn't done anything wrong. Except he had. He hadn't talked to her. He'd shut down the way he'd done before.

Except this time, hadn't she pushed him away, telling him that last night was never happening again?

She had. And he'd barely gotten a word in edgewise. She'd given him no chance to explain himself other than telling her the truth… that he was worried about hurting the babies. But maybe it went beyond that. Maybe calling Jessica was his way of making sure they actually *could* do more.

Maybe his "let's wait a little while" hadn't been an outright rejection, but a plea for some time to figure all this out.

But what was done was done. There was no going back on the way she'd slammed out of his office, was there? Yet if she didn't at least try, she might as well kiss any hope of repairing their relationship goodbye.

She would never know exactly how he felt, unless she sat down and talked to him rationally, not letting her hurt from the past come back and poison what they could have in the present…or the future. Looking at it from his perspective, maybe it had seemed the same way. That things had gotten turned around and she only wanted him as a provider of genetic material.

It was time to go back to him and find out what he wanted out of their marriage or at least know for sure if, as far as he was concerned, they were through. She would only know if she went and talked to him. Then, if there was even the smallest scrap of hope, they could go and meet with Jessica Lucas together and let her put Seb's mind at ease.

She went to the sink and rinsed out her glass, putting it on the rack beside the sink. She was tired and didn't really want to go all the way back to the hospital. But she didn't want to do this over the phone.

That sounded so familiar. She hadn't wanted to tell him about the babies over the phone, either.

So all she could do was drive back over there and find him and hopefully they could get away from the rush of the ER for a few minutes to have this out once and for all.

She turned to find her purse when a sharp pain went through her abdomen. She went still for a minute and held her breath, waiting to see if it happened again.

Okay, it had to just be a fluke. But when she went to take another step it hit again, and this time she felt moisture in her panties.

Dios. No. Please no. She held her hand over her midsection as she went into the bathroom, already knowing what she was going to find. Pulling her undergarment down, she looked and sure enough she was spotting. Just like she had earlier in her pregnancy. No. *No, no, no.* She wrapped her arms around her belly, trying to shield her babies from the unthinkable. Finally she forced herself to move. She needed to get help. Right now.

Her heart skipped a beat as she found an absorbent pad to put on. Surely the universe couldn't be that cruel. She was probably going to lose her marriage. Was some higher power really going to take her babies as well?

She hurried to the kitchen and got her phone out of her purse and pushed Seb's number, listening as it rang.

"Come on, Seb, answer, please!"

It went to voicemail. She didn't leave a message, simply tried the number again. They'd always had a system. If she called two times in a row, it was an emergency and he'd know to either pick up or call her right back.

The second call went to voicemail as well. She stared at the phone, willing him to return the call. Nothing happened.

She couldn't wait. He might be caught up in an emergency at work. Who knew how long it would take. So she called emergency services. Thank God they answered on the second ring. "What's your emergency?"

"I'm nearly five months pregnant with triplets and am having some spotting and pain." Her voice caught and she had to fight to get the rest of the words out. "Could you please send someone? And hurry!"

The dispatcher told her to go and lie down on her couch and that someone was on their way.

She went and unlocked her door, and when she went to turn away, another pain struck. Putting her hand to the spot, she somehow made it over to the couch and lay down. The relief was immediate. The pain disappeared. At least for now. She tried dialing Seb's number again, but there was still no response. She then tried calling the desk to the ER and without saying what was wrong asked if anyone had seen Seb.

"No, Bella, not in the last half hour or so. He's not down here on the floor."

"Okay, thanks."

She hung up. So he wasn't in the middle of an emergency. Where was he, and why wasn't he picking up? It wasn't like Seb, even if he was angry, to not answer her call.

She couldn't worry about that right now. She needed to worry about her babies. The pain had subsided, but she didn't dare get up and go look to see if there was any more spotting, so she did as the dispatcher had instructed and stayed on the couch.

The fifteen minutes until a knock sounded at the door seemed to take forever. "Come in," she called.

When the door opened and she saw Gabriel and his partner, an immediate sense of relief went through her. He and Seb were friends. He came over to the couch and knelt down beside it, putting his medical case on the floor. "What's going on, Bella?"

"I—I can't find Seb and..." She started to cry, and the pain immediately came back. She quickly stopped and took deep careful breaths. "I'm having pain in my abdomen and some spotting."

"How far along are you again?"

"Almost five months."

He nodded, but the concern on his face was obvious. "I'm going to get some vitals, and them I'm going to transfer you to the hospital."

"Okay. I've tried calling Seb several times, but there's been no answer."

"I'm sure he'll call you back any minute." Her sobs had subsided, but the tears hadn't and were now flowing in a silent stream down her face. Tears for herself. For Seb. And for their three precious babies.

Seb stood at the Greek bridge at the Bosques de Palermo and looked out over the water that he and Bella had been on two and a half weeks ago. There were several paddleboats in the water, and the sight made his chest ache. He should have been honest and told Bella that he'd wanted to call Jessica before actually having sex with her. But she'd been so frantic that he'd given in to her, being as gentle as he could. He knew if he'd given her what she wanted that he would have had a hard time holding himself back.

He'd called the doctor that morning as soon as he got into the office and she came right on the line and assured him it was fine, reiterating what she'd said at the appointment. They could have sex normally without fear at this point.

Then Bella had come into the office and had been so angry with him. He wasn't sure where all of it stemmed from, but he was pretty sure some of it was because he'd taken matters into his own hands rather than talking to her about it. Hadn't he tried to?

Maybe, but he hadn't told her he loved her since he'd gotten back from Africa. Because he was afraid she'd reject him. That she'd wanted him there only for the babies. But on the other hand, could it be that she was afraid of the very same thing? Of not being loved for herself apart from the babies?

How could she even doubt his love?

But if he didn't actually say the words, how was she ever going to know for sure? How would he know for sure? And he couldn't stay in the house if they didn't figure out a plan on where to go from here. She'd said they needed time apart. He'd thought the same thing at a certain point, but now he was more sure than ever that for both their sakes, they needed to know what the end goal for their relationship was. Stay together? Or separate for good?

Pushing away from the handrail of the

bridge, he reached in his back pocket for his phone to let her know he was headed back to the apartment only to find it wasn't there. Had he left it in the car?

Sometimes he tossed it on the console while he was driving so it didn't bother him while sitting in the seat. Hurrying back the way he'd come, he cursed the fact that the park suddenly seemed huge, the entrance so far away. Even sprinting part of the way, it still took him ten minutes to get back to the parking area. Once inside the car, he looked for his phone again and couldn't find it. He must have left it in his office. But the last thing he wanted to do was go all the way back there to get it. Besides, he wanted to talk to Bella in person and figure this out once and for all.

Starting the car, he headed back to the apartment.

When he arrived, he was glad to see that Bella's car was there, which meant she was there, too. Taking the elevator up, he got off and opened his front door, calling out for her. But there was no answer.

He called again. Nothing. Fear washed over him in a wave. Her vehicle was in the lot, so where was she? He searched the apartment and then looked in the bathroom. There was the strip from a woman's sanitary product in the trash can.

He went very still, staring at the item, a sense of panic coming over him. Had something gone wrong? And he'd left all over again, just like he had when he'd gone to Africa. He should have at least texted where he would be, in case she needed him.

He went to grab his keys off the table in the foyer and found a note.

Headed to the ER with Bella. She's spotting and having some pain. If you get this, meet us there. Gabriel.

He wasted no time, jumping back in his car and racing to the hospital. Although he knew it was due to the stress of not being able to get to her right away, the volume of traffic seemed so much heavier right now, the people in front of him so much slower than normal. But he finally arrived and parked in the closest spot he could find and rushed to the entrance.

He knew he had to look like a madman as he stood there desperately scouring the waiting area. One of the nurses came over to him and murmured, "She's in exam room one. They're waiting for Liz to finish up with an emergency C-section, and then she'll come in and check her over."

"Has anyone called Dr. Lucas yet?"

"Yes. She's also with a patient." The nurse touched his arm. "Just go be with her. That's the best thing you can do right now."

He nodded and headed back to where the exam rooms were, finding the right room and knocking before slipping inside.

Bella's head turned and when she saw him, she fell apart, sobbing into her hands. "Oh, Seb, I'm so sorry."

He didn't hesitate; he hopped onto the exam table next to her and wrapped his arms around her. "Hey. You have nothing to be sorry about."

"Maybe you were right about everything. Maybe we shouldn't have…"

"No. *You* were right. I called Jessica before you got to the office and she assured me that there wasn't much we could do to harm them."

"Then why is this happening to us again?" She buried her head in his chest. "Why now?"

"I don't know, honey. But I'm here. And babies or no babies, I'm going to stay right here beside you."

"But you made it pretty clear that you were only worried about them."

Her words were so muffled he wasn't sure what he was hearing at first. Then when her meaning broke through… God, how could she ever truly think that? "That's not true, Bella, and I'm sorry if I made you feel that way. What I'm terrified of is losing you. Of something going wrong. Of doing something that hurt not just the babies but you."

She leaned back to look up at him, her nose and eyes red from crying. "But you kept talking about them. Saying I needed to be careful. That we needed to be careful."

"Because you didn't seem to want me for anything but as support during your pregnancy, so that's what I became, even though it drove me crazy not to tell you I still loved you. That I never stopped loving you, even during that awful time before I left for Africa."

He tipped her face up. "I love these babies, but it's you I want. You I need. The babies are just a bonus package. I'm here for the duration, as long as it's what you want."

She closed her eyes for a second. "It is. I love you, too. And I'm sorry for putting you through all of those treatments. I know it wasn't what you wanted."

Is that what she really thought? If so, he had done a very poor job of showing her what was really important to him. "I hated seeing your devastation every time something went wrong. But I'm here to tell you, if you want ten children, I'll do everything in my power to see that you get them. But as far as what I need, it's you. It's always been you, Bella. I'm lost without you."

Liz swept into the room and took in the scene. "The front desk filled me in, but why don't you tell me what's going on."

Seb listened as Bella recounted that they'd made love yesterday. Then how today she and Seb had had a fight and she'd gone home and cried. She'd gotten up in an attempt to pull herself together and felt a sudden pain that made her double over. She'd then felt something wet in her panties and found that she'd spotted.

Seb took her hand and gave it a slight squeeze.

"When you say you spotted, was it a lot of blood or only a little?" Liz asked.

"Not a lot. It was more like mucus with a pink tinge. Not quite as much as what happened when the IVF treatments failed, but I was so afraid…"

"Are you still in pain?"

"When I twist to the right, it hurts. Yes."

"But no squeezing or cramping?"

"I don't think so."

"Let's take a look and see what's going on." Liz wheeled the ultrasound machine from its spot near the wall and brought it over to the bed. "Seb, can you help her get ready while I set up?"

He nodded. "Lie back, honey."

Bella did what he asked and he helped her slide her skirt down over her hips and unbuttoned her blouse. "Where did it hurt?"

She pointed to a spot on her right side, just below her rib cage. When he lightly pushed on the area, she tensed.

He caught Liz's eye. "I think it might be muscular, but I'll feel better once you see that the babies are all right."

Squeezing his wife's hand again, he leaned down and kissed her cheek.

She wrapped her arms around his neck and held him. "No matter what happens, I want you to know I love you. I want to make this marriage work."

A huge wave of emotion crashed through

him, and he closed his eyes and let himself be held tight. "Yes. We're going to make this work. No matter what happens." The moment seemed sacred, as if they were renewing their vows to each other.

"Are you ready?" Liz's voice reminded them that she was there, that there were still vital things that needed to be done.

Bella sucked down an audible breath before letting go of Seb and nodding.

She lay back on the bed, and Seb went to stand with her, holding her hand in his like they had the last time at Jessica Lucas's office. But this time was different. Because this time there was understanding between them in a way that there hadn't been for far too long.

Liz slid the wand back and forth over Bella's belly, looking for the babies. And when a sound filled the room—that strange cacophony of heartbeats that were not in sync with anything but each other, Seb's eyes burned. But not with sadness—it was a happiness that transcended anything he could understand.

"Do you hear that, Bell?"

She nodded, not saying anything, but her look said it all. She was incredibly relieved. "Are they all there?"

"I have Baby A, Baby B and Baby C, who is still neatly tucked behind Baby B, but not as much as he was."

Seb didn't correct her or tell her again which name went with which baby, because in the end it didn't matter. "They're all okay?"

"They seem to be. I don't see anything that could be cause for alarm at the moment. No problems with the placentas or babies, that I can tell."

"Why was I spotting, then?"

"It's not uncommon to spot. During the second trimester your cervix has a rich blood supply. Even an internal exam can cause some light spotting. It's benign in a lot of cases. As far as the pain goes, I'll send Jessica a note and let her know what happened, but I think Seb was right about it being muscular. I'm not seeing any evidence of uterine contractions, so I'm going to chalk that up to a strained muscle."

"I don't want you working today. Either of you." She glanced at him. "Go home and pamper her, Seb. Jessica will probably give you a call sometime today to check on you. I will as well. If you spot again or if the flow turns heavier, come back in immediately. Okay?"

"We will."

"Here's some tissues to clean your belly up." Liz gave her a quick hug. "You know you can call me anytime, right?"

"I do, thank you so much."

The ob-gyn shook hands with Seb. "You guys take as long as you need in here."

"Thanks again."

As soon as Liz left the room, Seb took the box of tissues and gently cleared away the lubricant from Bella's abdomen. Then he helped her readjust her clothing. "Can I lie beside you for a few minutes?"

She nodded, and Seb climbed into the bed with her and tucked his arm beneath her shoulders. "What are you thinking?"

She turned sideways on the bed and snuggled into him. "I'm thinking that I can't believe how lucky I am. And how stupid."

"Stupid?"

"To have let things between us get as bad as they were. I should have told you sooner that I still loved you, but I was afraid I'd killed whatever you'd felt toward me."

He kissed her forehead. "I was afraid of the same thing." He needed to clear the air about one item. "I shouldn't have gone to Africa. Looking back, I realize how utterly selfish it was of me."

She lifted her head to look at him. "No, you did what you needed to do. And honestly, I think I needed to get an up-close-and-personal look at what I stood to lose. Because when I saw you standing there in a mass of feathers the day you returned to Buenos Aires, I suddenly realized I didn't want to lose you. It was one of the scariest days of my life, because I thought I already had."

Bella dropped a kiss on his chin. "I hope you're happy as the father of three, because I won't be trying for anymore."

"Are you sure? We could adopt."

"We could. Or we could volunteer for some programs for disadvantaged kids."

He stroked the side of her face. "As long as we do it together, I'm open to almost anything."

Her mouth twisted sideways. "Not anything, as we saw last night."

"Last night I was worried. And I'm still worried. I want to talk to Jessica again before going any further than we did in bed yesterday, in light of what happened today. I think I may have caused your spotting."

"You heard Liz. It's nothing. Just extra blood vessels. Besides, we don't have to do a repeat of last night. I'm anxious to finish what I started."

"What do you mean?"

"I mean you interrupted me at the best part when we first got inside the apartment."

He grinned before shaking his head. "As sexy as that sounds, do you mind if we just curl up and watch some TV? I just want to be near you. I just want to sit on the couch and not have a cloud hanging over my head. Just enjoy being *us* again…being together. Do you think we could manage that?"

"I think we could manage that." She leaned forward and kissed him on the mouth. "I am so very lucky, Seb. And I promise I won't take it for granted again. Ever."

"I won't either. I love you, Bell."

"Love you, too."

He sat up, pulling her with him. "So, are we ready to get out of here and go home?"

"Yes. Let's go home."

He stopped. "Wait. I need to do something first."

"What's that?"

"I need to find out where the hell I left my cell phone. I'm never going to be without it for the rest of the pregnancy. I almost died when

I saw the note Gabriel left, couldn't get here fast enough."

"Is it in our office?"

"I'm pretty sure it is. I left from there and went straight to the park to think. And then I stopped home to tell you what I'd realized—that I love you, babies or no babies. And I mean that."

"Same here. I love you, too, babies or no babies. But I sure am glad we have them."

He slid off the table. "So am I. So let's never fight again."

"I can't promise that, because remember what used to happen when we would fight?"

He smiled. "Makeup sex?"

She laughed. "Makeup sex. Wasn't it the best?"

"*Mi amor*, everything with you is the best."

"Let's find that phone and get home. Oh, and you will be moving back into our room, right?"

"Yes. Starting tonight and every night thereafter."

She wrapped her arms around him and reached up to receive his kiss. "Tonight and every night thereafter."

EPILOGUE

Three years later

BELLA SAT ON the huge picnic blanket and watched as their three boys wrestled with their dad on a grassy stretch of the Bosques de Palermo. This place had been "the destination" ever since the triplets were born. They'd gone from being wheeled in huge ungainly strollers to now, when the little guys could manage it on their sturdy little legs. They'd yet to do the paddleboats with them, for safety reasons, but every once in a while, she and Seb would hire a sitter and come out here by themselves and rent one.

Then they would make out under the bridge, not caring who saw them.

Seb had still wanted to be cautious about having sex while she was pregnant, but she'd made him promise that once the boys were born they could be as adventurous as they wanted to be in that area. And he had *not* disappointed. The man not only had ideas, but he had *ideas*. Their sex life was rich and full and wonderful. As was every other part of their life.

And as much as she was embarrassed to admit it, lying together on the couch after they'd put the trio to bed and quietly watching a movie had become the highlight of her nights. Seb said it was his as well.

They'd had to sell their apartment and buy something bigger, as they soon outgrew the two-bedroom place, but their new apartment was in the same complex and so it had been an easy move. And it held none of the painful memories of loss that their old place had.

So many things at the hospital had changed, but some others hadn't. She and Seb still led the emergency department, but her hours had been shortened by a quarter so that she could be home for the boys when they finished preschool. And she'd politicked for Mario Soldado, the patient whose hands had had to be amputated due to electrical burns, to lead talks on the very real dangers of electrocution and ways to avoid it.

She'd heard inklings of new and rekindled

romances, but Bella was too busy with her own romance with Seb to listen to the rumors that always circulated around the hospital. She just wished everyone the same happiness that she and Seb had found together.

"Okay, guys, are you ready to eat?"

Four male faces turned her way, and her eyes went down the line, loving each and every member of her family from Luis, who was still the littlest of the triplets, but who was catching up with his brothers, to her hunky husband, who would always be her hero. They'd even talked about going on a Doctors without Borders assignment together when the kids were a little older. There was no reason not to anymore. She wanted to be wherever Seb was.

She passed out plates of cold chicken, fruit and a fluffy chocolate mousse to everyone and watched them eat with gusto. The boys got chocolate everywhere, but that was one of the parts of being a mom that she loved the most. Watching their enjoyment each and every day.

Seb's dad was still cancer-free and had loved their trip to Scotland. So had Helena. They planned one day to all go together.

Bella had no idea what the future held for any of them, but as long as they were together, how could it be anything but good? Just like their joint prayer before bedtime that had ended with what had become the motto for their life: tonight and every night thereafter.

* * * * *

Look out for the next story in the Buenos Aires Docs quartet

Surgeon's Brooding Brazilian Rival
by Luana DaRosa

And if you enjoyed this story, check out these other great reads from Tina Beckett

Tempting the Off-Limits Nurse
A Daddy for the Midwife's Twins?
Resisting the Brooding Heart Surgeon

All available now!